ordeal when a hunted terrorist crosses their path . . .

www.

Also available in the Alpha Force series:

SURVIVAL

RAT-CATCHER

DESERT PURSUIT

HOSTAGE

RED CENTRE

BLOOD MONEY

Coming soon:

BLACK GOLD

FAULT LINE

UNTOUCHABLE

RED CENTRE

RED
FOX

Papers used by Random House Children's Books are natural, recyclable products made from wood grown in sustainable forests. The manufacturing processes conform to the environmental regulations of the country of origin.

Typeset in Sabon by Palimpsest Book Production Limited, Polmont, Stirlingshire

Red Fox Books are published by Random House Children's Books, 61–63 Uxbridge Road, London W5 5SA, a division of The Random House Group Ltd, in Australia by Random House Australia (Pty) Ltd, 20 Alfred Street, Milsons Point, Sydney, NSW 2061, Australia, in New Zealand by Random House New Zealand Ltd, 18 Poland Road, Glenfield, Auckland 10, New Zealand, and in South Africa by Random House (Pty) Ltd, Endulini, 5A Jubilee Road, Parktown 2193, South Africa

THE RANDOM HOUSE GROUP Limited Reg. No. 954009
www.**kidsatrandomhouse**.co.uk

A CIP catalogue record for this book is available from the British Library.

Printed and bound in Great Britain by Cox & Wyman Ltd, Reading, Berkshire

Author photograph © Colin Thomas
Cover image, Getty Images by Art Wolfe

ALPHA FORCE

The field of operation...

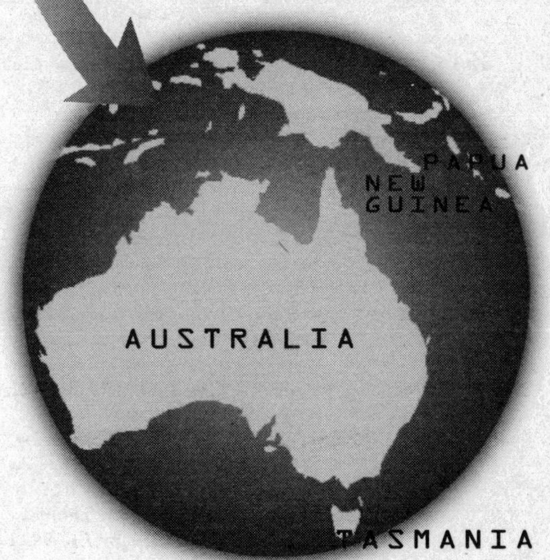

1
Fun and Games

Being up the tree wasn't the scary part. It was OK if you looked straight ahead at what was in front of your nose. All you saw was the trunk, which was solid, gnarled and rough, with warty areas like the hide of a prehistoric animal. In places Hex could see tiny cracks, where a softer, redder substance showed through the bark. It smelled warm and woody and wet. In fact everywhere was warm and wet. Hex's clothes were drenched with sweat and when he breathed in, the air was damp like steam.

The trouble started if you looked anywhere

but straight ahead. Not down – Hex knew better than to look down – but on either side. Then he saw thin air and foliage fading into a blue haze in the far distance and his senses started turning somersaults.

He felt his teeth baring in a fierce grin that was outside his control. It was partly nervousness, partly a sense of the absurdity of his position. Here he was, suspended ten metres up a red cedar tree in the Australian rainforest with his foot on a branch, waiting for the signal to swing on a rope to the next tree. A week earlier Hex hadn't even realized Australia had thick jungles like this. Now he knew – thanks to an online virtual tour while waiting to board his plane – that the vast continent harboured a great variety of terrains, and many extremes. Here at the very tip of the Daintree Rainforest in Queensland all was lush, wet and tropical. Hex knew that only ten or so kilometres away, the land became arid and the trees shrivelled to scrub and bush.

Hex focused on the tree he was clinging to, then swivelled his head slowly like an owl, careful not to risk a disorientating glance up or down. His gaze found the next tree, his destination. A bright yellow star-shaped target glittered there, pinned between two branches.

Together with four friends from far-flung corners of the globe, Hex was part of the group they called Alpha Force. They had tackled many arduous missions together but this had to be one of the strangest – volunteering to try out a series of games for a reality TV show. It's for charity, Hex reminded himself soberly, forcing the grin off his face before it turned into hysteria. For every star collected, a sponsor would pay money to a chosen charity, and so Alpha Force were here doing a trial run before the real contestants arrived.

Hex wasn't entirely in his element. The kind of games he excelled at involved codes and were firmly grounded in cyberspace: he was an expert hacker and code-breaker. His natural habitat was indoors, at his computer or in the gym. When he wasn't on a mission with Alpha Force, the only contact he had with the great outdoors was running and cycling across Hampstead Heath. But here he was, hanging up a tree in a steamy rainforest, waiting for the camera crew to finalize their positions and lighting.

The other members of Alpha Force weren't having it any easier. As Hex was edging his feet nervously along the branch, his Anglo-Chinese friend Li was hurtling towards the ground twenty metres away at the end of a bungee rope. Unlike Hex, though, Li most definitely *was* in her element. She was grasping the rope with both hands with her knees bent and her feet out ready for the impact. The moment she touched down on the forest floor, she folded at the waist and knees and then sprang up like a cat, propelling herself towards a box high up in another tree. The move was graceful and smooth, and executed with the pinpoint accuracy of one who has trained as an athlete from an early age. The tight plait of Li's long black silky hair sailed out behind her like a tail and her slim legs caught a branch with the ease of a trapeze artist. She wrapped her legs around it and steadied herself while she reached into the box for one of the yellow stars. Then, like a monkey, she dropped back down to the ground and lifted off again in one slick movement.

Paulo would have been happy right then to have joined his friends in the trees. He was on his hands and knees in a Perspex tunnel which was like a greenhouse in the fierce Australian heat. Brushing sweat out of his eyes with his wrist, Paulo came across one of the yellow stars and grabbed it, eager to finish the game trial and get back out into fresh air – or, at any rate, fresher air; the whole rainforest was like a sauna at this time of day. On Paulo's list of priorities right at that moment, saving the tiger from extinction ran a distant second to gulping down an ice-cold cola float.

Paulo lifted the target. 'Got it!' he called to the camera crew.

The first thing that hit him was an angry droning noise. On the earth in front of him, a black shape was spreading like treacle. Was it tar? Oil? Paulo had a split-second when he noted with curiosity that the black stuff glinted with a blue metallic sheen, and then a cloud of huge flies hurtled up into his face like missiles. They buzzed around his ears and pelted his skin, seeking out the sweat that dripped off him in a constant flow. He let out a splutter and they swarmed into his open mouth. He felt a crunching sensation, a bitter taste, and spat violently, shaking his head and then his whole body in an effort to dislodge them. Crunched flies stuck between his lips and teeth. The walls of the tunnel rocked from side to side. It made no difference. The flies were glued to the sweat on his face like a black lace veil. They began to swarm down under his collar and creep up his sleeves.

Paulo had reckoned he was fairly used to flies: on his ranch in Argentina flies and other insects were a constant torment to the livestock and the people who handled them. But this was something else.

'Who dreams up TV shows like this anyway?' he muttered under his breath as he crawled doggedly on into the next chamber. This was hung with spider webs. Maybe webs were just what he needed to deal with the flies, Paulo thought.

The webs stuck to him like sticky muslin, but he barely noticed against all the droning and fizzing in his ears. He lifted the next target and under it was a large spider.

Paulo grimaced at the spider. 'I'll swap you that star for all these delicious flies – how about that?' he said.

'Hold it there, Paulo,' called one of the camera technicians. 'We need to set up the close-up on the spider. Won't take a second.'

Paulo waited, grumbling to himself in his native Spanish. He wasn't too squeamish about wildlife, but this spider wasn't exactly his first choice of company in a confined space. Its body was dark and torpedo-shaped and marked with fine yellow flecks. Its legs were as long as Paulo's fingers and sported yellow bands. They shifted and fidgeted and Paulo imagined hypodermic needles ready to offload poison. Not that it would really be poisonous, of course. Not in a TV game show; Paulo knew that. He just had to keep telling himself.

'Sorry, Paulo,' called the technician. 'This is going to take longer than we thought. Make yourself comfortable.'

'Looks like we're stuck with each other,' Paulo told the spider wryly. 'Got any yarns you'd like to spin while we wait?'

Alex meanwhile was also crawling – even more uncomfortably. He was on his hands and knees in a trench that had been turned into a miniature swamp, complete with weeds and leeches – and an authentically rank smell. As Alex moved along he felt the bottom for the tell-tale hard edges of a yellow star. Actually, although the trench was most people's idea of hell, Alex didn't find it too unpleasant. It reminded him of stories his father had told him. Alex's dad was in the SAS, and survival lore – along with deliciously hair-raising stories of SAS selection – had been as natural a part of Alex's upbringing and education as football and double maths.

Alex's fingers found a target under the mud and he yanked it up, pulling it free of the weeds. The mud slurped thickly and released a pungent gust of gas – a clammy, rotting smell that caught the back of Alex's throat and made him gag. He paused and closed his eyes tightly, willing the nausea to pass. His dad had once told him how he had had to crawl through a sewer on a covert mission in Colombia – or maybe it was after a night on the tiles in Glasgow? Either way, Alex told himself he would have to be prepared for anything if he was to follow in his father's footsteps.

The mud was up to his shoulders and hips at this point and felt like thick warm slurry inside his T-shirt and shorts, but Alex looked on the bright side: at least it kept the mosquitoes away. He paused and slicked some of the mud over his face and neck like camouflage cream. This would be heaven if I was a hippo, he thought.

A short time later, the fifth member of the team, Amber, was wading chest-deep in a lake a few hundred metres away, making her way towards a clump of reeds where she could see a star target. Fronds of water weed brushed against her bare legs and occasionally she felt something more solid slither past, but that might have been her imagination. She was wearing her walking boots, so she felt fairly well protected. On the whole she was finding the games good fun. The lake formed an open clearing in the heart of the jungle, and Amber was enjoying being out in the sun, her black skin soaking up the rays greedily. It was the first time she'd seen the sun since Alpha Force had arrived in the rainforest the day before. So far they'd stayed under the immense canopy of trees; even at high noon it was like a dark, damp underworld. The green light filtering in shifting patterns through the leaves had reminded her of scuba-diving in the gloom of the ocean floor. Now she felt as if she had swum up and broken through the surface.

Water was a natural habitat for Amber. She was as much at home *on* water as *in* it. Her parents had been software billionaires and had owned several yachts. As well as being an expert sailor, she was proficient at all water sports, skiing, horse riding and archery. After her parents had died in a plane crash, Amber had discovered that they were a good deal more adventurous than she had ever imagined. Secretly they had put their skills and wealth to good use, exposing human rights abuses and smuggling film from oppressive regimes to newsrooms around the world. Amber had led a sheltered rich-kid existence up till then. Now she, like Alex, was determined to uphold the family tradition.

As Amber untangled the first target, she caught sight of Hex at the water's edge. He must have finished his game. Let's see how alert he is, she thought. With a flick of the wrist she frisbeed the target out of the lake.

Hex caught it in a smooth movement. 'You throw like a girl,' he shouted.

'Yeah? You catch like a geek,' said Amber, flashing him a grin.

Tracey, a production executive in her early twenties, was standing on the bank waving her wide-brimmed bush hat. 'Over there, Amber.'

Amber looked round. There was a second yellow star on a rock a little way off. She set off towards it, wading purposefully.

On the bank, Hex tapped Tracey on the shoulder. 'Excuse me, but have you seen that?' He pointed to a clump of reeds. A crocodile skulked low in the water, its rough back glistening in the sun like a wet log. Its half-closed eye was just visible above the water line.

Tracey looked up from her clipboard and peered at Hex over the top of her rimless glasses. 'It's not a real crocodile,' she said in a laboriously patient tone, as if talking to a small child rather than a teenager with genius-level IQ. She pointed to other dark shapes in the water. 'Look – there, and there. They're just props. Plastic.'

'I can see those other ones are plastic,' replied Hex. 'But I just came up from that direction and there wasn't a crocodile there then.'

Tracey gave him a condescending smile. 'They're plastic,' she said again. 'That means they float, and they tend to drift around a bit once people wade in and start stirring up the water.'

Another target came whizzing across. Hex caught it on reflex, even though he hadn't been looking. As he turned, he noticed a couple of men in green ranger uniforms standing near the water's edge holding what looked like tranquillizer guns.

'Smart catch,' said Tracey.

'Are they for authenticity too?' said Hex, nodding towards the men.

'Yes, we're going to use them during filming. It makes the audience think it's all for real, you see.'

Amber was wading towards a third star target when she stopped abruptly.

Hex instantly tensed. Something caused the hairs on his neck to prickle. 'Amber, you OK?' he called.

'My foot's stuck in some weed,' replied Amber. Hex could see her shoulders jerk as she pulled hard. But she didn't move. 'Darn,' she muttered. 'Must be caught on my boot.' She jerked her foot again, harder.

Hex's uneasy feeling hadn't gone away. He looked over to the crocodile again. It looked much the same as it had before. Or did it? Hex had an excellent eye for detail. He could explore high security computer systems and erase all trace that he had been there. He had learned to trust his instincts. *Think*, he told himself. *What's wrong with this picture?*

He looked at the other crocs. They were just as low in the water as the one he'd noticed, moving from side to side in the ripples created as Amber tried to pull her foot free.

And then Hex realized what was wrong. All the other crocodiles were moving. But this one was dead still. It was real! It had sensed that Amber was in trouble and was stalking her.

In the water, Amber swore again, took a deep breath and sank below the surface.

Hex yelled at the top of his lungs, 'Amber, no!'

In the murky depths, Amber didn't hear him. She couldn't see a thing either. She had kicked up so much silt that the water was like vegetable soup. She groped around her ankle and felt the rope-like weed that had snared her foot. Her fingers explored it and she found a thick section, with some thinner fronds that had caught on the hooks of her boots. She was stuck fast.

Breathing out hard, Amber surfaced. The first thing she heard was Hex shouting furiously: 'Amber! Get out of the water! There's a crocodile!'

Amber's head shot round. She saw Hex waving his arms frantically, while Tracey was rooted to the spot. Next to them, the rangers were raising tranquillizer guns to their shoulders. Her heart pounding, Amber followed the line of the barrels and saw a dark shape, low in the water. She yanked her foot hard but it remained tethered to the bottom. She was helpless – an animal in a trap.

Tracey was crying, her voice hysterical. 'It's no good. The guns aren't loaded yet!'

'It's my boot,' shrieked Amber. 'I'm going to try to get it off.'

Hex saw Amber sink down again. Keeping her head above the water, she was feeling for her boot-laces. Her face was a mask of desperation as she scrabbled to undo them. Hex knew the type of boots Amber wore. They were built for strenuous outdoor hiking, durable as Kevlar and tightly fixed around her ankles with criss-crossed lacing. When the others were waiting for Amber to get ready, they often complained about how fiddly those boots were. 'That's the whole point,' she always said. 'I know they aren't going to come off in a hurry.'

Now those reliable boots had become a death trap.

'The croc's gone,' said one of the rangers. He lowered his gun warily.

'It's underwater somewhere,' said the other ranger.

Amber's fingers must have worked like lightning. She was free of her boot and powering towards them in a strong front crawl.

'Go, Amber, go!' shrilled Tracey. She was jumping up and down in almost a cartoon parody of panic.

With a hungry crocodile in the water behind her, Amber needed no encouragement. She hit the lake edge, and all eyes were on her as she splashed through the reeds and out onto the shore. Weals showed bright red on her dark skin where her leg had been cut into by the cable-hard weeds. She scrabbled across the mud and collapsed at Hex's feet, gasping.

'Where is it . . . ?'

Tracey stepped closer to the water's edge and peered down. 'It's gone,' she said. She turned and looked back at them with a smile. 'Vanished. We must have scared it off.'

Realization hit Hex like a thunderbolt. He moved back, dragging Amber with him. 'Get away from the edge!' he shrieked. 'Get away!'

Tracey turned, puzzled. At that moment the water beside her exploded as the crocodile erupted from the lake like a missile. Hex saw the great hinged jaws outlined in a spray of water. It was a sight to inspire shock and awe: a gaping prehistoric mouth filled with uneven reptile fangs. It was a frozen fragment of time, an uncanny glimpse into a Jurassic morning.

Adrenaline made Hex move like Max Payne in bullet time. He seized one of the useless tranquillizer guns. Swinging it directly over his head like a kendo stick, he brought it down with all his strength. The blow landed solidly on the soft part of the crocodile's nose. The reptile twisted round, still with a fixed expression of cold-blooded glee, and hit the water with a heavy splash.

'Run!' yelled Hex. This time nobody bothered to ask questions. As one, the party raced for the tree line. Hex knew that the croc might possibly follow them onto the lake shore, but one glance back told him that it had had enough. It was heading back towards the centre of the lake.

Then they stood, leaning on trees, panting and gasping, as they got their breath back. Tracey was on all fours, her stomach heaving in and out like bellows, her eyes wide and horrified.

Amber fell to her knees and then rolled onto her backside. 'Ow, my foot,' she yelped, sitting up and inspecting her bare sole. 'I've trodden on something I shouldn't have.'

One of the rangers looked at her. 'I thought you'd had it there, girl.'

Hex stretched out flat on the ground and let out a long sigh. 'It wasn't Amber it wanted after all. It was more interested in the people standing on the shore.'

'I feel quite offended,' said Amber, laughing in sheer relief. 'What is it? Don't I look tasty? Not enough fat on me, or what?'

'Oh my God,' said Tracey to Hex. 'You just saved our lives.'

'Yeah . . .' Amber looked at him, shaking her head slowly. 'How did you know to do that?'

'I thought I'd better learn a martial art so I took advantage of a cut-price, fourteen-day holiday at the Shaolin Temple,' said Hex.

Amber gave him her sternest look.

Hex propped himself up on his elbow and grinned. 'OK, I saw it in a game.'

They were all quiet for a moment. Then Amber said brightly, 'Well, the next game is to find my lost boot. Any volunteers?'

2
Friends Reunited

The rainforest was serenading the sunset.

Barely fifteen degrees off the equator, night falls quickly. In less time than it took to get the campfire blazing, the soft green light had thickened to blackness. It was as though a stage curtain had been lowered around the camp.

And then the noise started. Every frog, bird, insect and animal within twenty miles had begun to sing, chirrup, rasp, hoot, click and caw. It was the most deafening natural sound that any of Alpha Force could recall. They sat on logs around a fire, while a stew of chicken and vegetables bubbled gently in front of them.

'It's incredible,' said Hex, whose knowledge of the world, though extensive, came mainly from what he had read and seen on the Web. Real experiences never failed to astonish and delight him – the outward manifestation, as Hex saw it, of an underlying mathematical pattern.

'I thought a night under the stars would be peaceful,' shouted Paulo. 'But this is as deafening as any nightclub!'

Alex smiled and cupped his ear. It was almost impossible to hear, so the five of them sat in silence, their conversation drowned out by the din. Each was left with his or her own thoughts.

When Alex had arrived the day before, his first stop after checking in at the hotel was the gym. As with the other members of Alpha Force, exercise had become a way of life for him, and he constantly tried to increase his strength and stamina and learn new skills. After the long, soporific journey that had started in Northumberland and ended in Queensland, he was stiff and bristling with pent-up energy, and he planned a workout in a cool air-conditioned gym to get the kinks out. Alex found Hex already there on the treadmill. Pretty soon, Li bounded in wearing micro-shorts and hurtled over to ambush the two boys with a bear hug that they pretended to find embarrassing. When Paulo and Amber arrived, itching to get moving after their flights from America, Alpha Force was complete for the first time this holiday.

They set up an impromptu circuit. The gym superviser stopped reading his fitness magazine and began to watch with interest as one of them ran on the treadmill, three of them sparred on the mats, and the other did press-ups and sit-ups with a medicine ball. He had never seen teenagers exercise so diligently. After a few minutes they took a thirty-second break and swapped to a different activity. After several circuits, the first rush of exuberant energy now burned off, they started to get their second wind.

Alex and Hex took to the treadmills. On the mats, Li spun and flip-flopped past them, doing a variety of Arab springs, tumbles and back-flips. Amber and Paulo, both expert horse riders with excellent balance, found a pair of FitBalls that looked like giant beach balls. They stood upright on the balls and trundled them along the length of the gym, hooting with laughter as they wobbled furiously to and fro. Hex tried it too, managed to walk his ball forward a few inches, and then tumbled off spectacularly to land smack on the mat. Commandeering his ball, Li was soon bowling along, her acrobatic prowess giving her the edge.

Only when they started to warm down, getting their heart rates back to normal and stretch their muscles, did the jet lag finally start to creep up on them. Amber was stretching her back in a yoga pose when she started feeling very sleepy. She looked around and laughed when she saw Alex yawning, his grey eyes screwed up and his blond fringe flopping over his forehead. Li, folded up in the lotus position with her head on the floor, her black hair in an inky pool around her, looked as though she was on the point of dozing off. Paulo and Hex, helping each other with hamstring stretches, were struggling to keep their eyes open.

Alex clapped his hands. 'C'mon, guys, let's get some rest. Big day tomorrow.'

They had hauled themselves upright with an effort and went up to spend their last night on soft beds with cotton sheets. Tomorrow they were bound for the rainforest, and three days of hammocks and waterproof sleeping bags in a makeshift camp on the edge of the competition area. The campsite area for the actual celebrity contestants was still being finalized but Alpha Force would be camping out in an out-of-the-way area, leaving no trace afterwards that they had been there. This, of course, meant camping with minimal equipment. Catching up would have to wait until they had the basics set up.

Gradually the sunset cacophony subsided.

Paulo was first to speak. 'As I was saying before I was so rudely interrupted, this spider was enormous . . .' His brown eyes twinkled as he told his story. He got up and lobbed another log onto the fire; it sent a shower of crackling red sparks up into the night sky.

Li selected a cooking pot for the rice, checking it for wildlife before filling it with water. She looked sceptically at Paulo, her eyes narrowed. 'So, this spider – you're saying it was black, with little yellow spots and a yellow band on each leg?'

Paulo nodded. 'Great long legs. This long.' He found a couple of twigs ten centimetres long in the pile of kindling and walked them along the ground.

'It's an orb spider. It's harmless.' Li sniggered. 'Unless you're ticklish.' She looked over at Paulo mischievously, and then twitched as though something had run up her sleeve. 'Ooh, I feel all itchy.'

The joke struck a nerve. Paulo shuddered, a movement that ran through his body from top to toe. It didn't take much to make him remember the feeling, but he refused to give Li the satisfaction of seeing him scratch.

'Ow, ooh,' chortled Li. 'What's that crawling in my hair? It tickles.'

Paulo tried to concentrate on sorting wood for kindling, putting out of his mind the uncomfortable notion that some of the flies might have crawled into his inner ear to spend the night.

'When I saw this guy earlier,' said Alex, building the fire, 'he was covered in flies. There were more than a jeans warehouse, I'm telling you. You looked like the inside of an Eccles cake, Paulo.'

'Urgh, gross,' exclaimed Amber. She was making a circuit of the camp, driving slim stakes of wood into the ground near each of the camp beds. They would be useful later for hanging boots and clothes on when they went to bed. Anything left in contact with the ground would probably be damp and full of wildlife by the morning.

Damp was almost as much of a problem as the flora and fauna. They were all constantly dripping with sweat in the humid atmosphere and Hex was worried about his palmtop. He had wrapped it in a sock to absorb moisture, and then in a plastic bag, before stowing it carefully in its carrying case.

'No, Eccles cakes are nice,' replied Alex. He was lighting a new fire with a spill. He bent down and blew on it until it caught, then brought over some more logs and put them to dry.

'I don't know about Eccles cakes, *amigo*,' said Paulo. 'But after your game you looked like a mud pie!'

Amber used a twig to brush away a hairy caterpillar that had found its way onto her camp bed. 'I hope these aren't on the menu tonight.' She curled her lip. 'I draw the line at eating grubs and creepy crawlies.'

Hex moved close to Amber and said in a low voice, 'Did you get your foot seen to? You have to be careful. Did you tell the TV people—?'

'Course I did, code boy,' said Amber, rolling her eyes. Any wound could become infected in a jungle environment, but Amber was a diabetic, which meant she might not heal as quickly as normal. Cuts on her hands and feet had to be treated with great care, and she had learned to be meticulous about her medication. Everywhere she went she carried glucose tablets and insulin injector pens in a small leather pouch.

Coming up to Paulo as she completed her circuit of the camp, she paused and reached down into his curly mop of hair, pretending to pluck out an insect. 'Got it!'

Paulo swatted her away. 'Pack it in, you guys,' he said, although he had to use considerable willpower not to start scratching.

There was a kind of contentment in the way they all worked together as a team, quietly and efficiently, anticipating each other's needs. The rudiments of building a camp were as familiar to Alpha Force as their ABC, and they had replayed this scenario in so many different ways in remote areas all over the world. Usually they wouldn't be looking forward to chicken stew and rice; more commonly it would be boil-in-the-bag rations in foil containers. If they were lucky, they would have them hot; but if it was impossible to light a fire, they would eat them cold. When they were together, their other lives – studying in places as diverse as Argentina and inner London – seemed to belong to different people. Now, all that seemed to exist for Li, Alex, Amber, Paulo and Hex was a cooking fire surrounded by their camp beds and a forest ticking with wildlife. It could be anywhere, and now they were all together it felt very much like home.

After supper Li handed round mugs of eucalyptus tea, made in a billycan from a sprig of eucalyptus plucked from a nearby tree.

Alex sniffed his with suspicion. 'What's this for? I haven't got a cold.'

'It's refreshing, you moron,' replied Li, and drew in the vapour with relish. Alex didn't look convinced.

'So, Amber, I didn't get what your uncle's connection is with all this . . .' said Hex.

John Middleton, Amber's uncle, had been her parents' anchor man and financier, and had helped the five friends set up Alpha Force. Now history was repeating itself as he provided back-up for their covert operations. Although he wasn't entirely happy about his niece getting involved in dangerous missions, he realized it had given her a new lease of life. She had an outlet for her energy and intelligence, and it helped to ease the pain of losing her parents. He had an extensive network of contacts which he used to arrange training for the five friends.

'It was through an old news colleague of my folks,' said Amber. 'Mum and Dad smuggled him several exclusives over the years. He's now in TV production and needed some guinea pigs to try out the games here so that the camera crew could sort out the angles. Uncle John thought it might be a way to brush up on our survival skills in a situation that was a little less dangerous than some of our missions.'

Hex grimaced. 'Less dangerous? Funny, that,' he said.

Amber smiled ruefully. 'Yes, I'll think twice before volunteering for a nice safe water game again.'

Paulo leaned forwards and peered at her intently, frowning. 'Volunteered? You mean you got to volunteer? Amber, if I ever find out you had anything to do with my ending up in a spider case for half an hour, covered in spiders' favourite food, I'll pour bees in your ears.' He turned to Alex and grinned. 'What do you say, Alex? Did you enjoy your swamp crawl?'

Alex was looking thoughtful. He smiled to himself, as though what Paulo said had echoed a private joke.

Paulo read the expression at once. 'Come on, Alex, what are you thinking? Spill the beans.'

Alex took a breath. 'Well, I was thinking I might have to do that sort of thing soon anyway. I've applied to join the army. I've been to see them and I had to do some exams and aptitude tests; then there were lectures about the regiments.'

Although Alex usually kept himself to himself, he began to warm to his subject. His face became more and more animated in the firelight as he spoke. 'In a year I could be patrolling in Bosnia or Kosovo, or applying for the Paras. Whatever I do, eventually I'll want to have a crack at getting into the SAS, of course. But that's a bit of a way off and I'll have to work hard – they don't just take anyone.'

In the darkness they could hear the lone cry of a rainforest animal. Normally nothing ventured out at night, and the sound seemed desolate and lost.

Li was the first to break the silence. 'Gosh, I haven't really thought about what I'll be doing next,' she said.

Li rarely made a remark that wasn't laced with mischief. Amber felt uncomfortable – she wanted to break the solemn mood that had suddenly settled over them. 'Hey, Paulo,' she said lightly, 'are you sure there aren't still some flies in that hair of yours? Just think of all those tiny feet, feelers and mandibles prickling inside your clothes!'

This time Paulo couldn't resist. He just had to have a scratch.

3

A Face from the Past

It was a small town on a coastal road, where the towering green jungle gave way to a sparkling sea. Along one side of the road lay the beach, sand stretching for miles like a golden ribbon between the emerald of the jungle and the sapphire waters of Cape Tribulation. Further out to sea was the Great Barrier Reef. Inland, the rainforest climbed steeply up the mountain, trees waving gently in the coastal breeze. On the road the sun, no longer shielded by the canopy of trees, beat down ferociously and fine drifts of white sand stirred on the baked black surface.

The town nestled in the foothills – really no more than a shop and a filling station, alongside a handful of isolated houses. The shop was a general store that also sold survival and sailing gear. One night in the jungle camp had made it very clear to the five members of Alpha Force that they needed more insect repellant, tarpaulins and water containers.

'Especially the insect repellant,' Li reminded everyone as she scratched the gnat bites on her wrists and ankles.

Amber was trying on some new boots. 'They're not nearly as snug as my American ones,' she complained.

'That's because you haven't broken them in,' said Hex.

Amber, threading the laces, paused and gave him an exasperated look. 'I know that, dumb ass. But I've just lost my favourite boots. I want to moan about it a bit.'

Alex and Li were debating the merits of a survival belt, hung with pockets and clips. Paulo, bored, leaned against the open façade at the front of the store and watched the blue surf surge in.

A man left the checkout and walked past Paulo with a paper bag of supplies under his arm. There was something about him that held Paulo's interest. He looked familiar somehow, but Paulo couldn't work out why. He wasn't one of the technical crew they'd hitched a ride with. Paulo wondered if he might have seen him at the hotel. But no, that wasn't it.

Attention to detail was second nature to all of Alpha Force. Paulo studied the man as he paused on the porch to slide on his sunglasses. He was of medium height, with a slightly heavy build that came from a lack of condition. Paulo glanced up to get a glimpse of his face in the security mirror by the door and saw dark Mediterranean features, the hair flecked with threads of grey.

The man hefted his grocery bag and walked across the car park. It was then that the hairs stood up on Paulo's neck. Now he knew where he'd seen him before.

The man had a slightly uneven walk, as though one hip didn't work as well as the other. Having spent his life with horses and cattle, Paulo noticed abnormalities in the way they moved – it was often the only clue to the fact that they had an injury. With humans too, he was often able to tell if someone had a back or knee problem from watching the way they walked. Paulo was sure he had seen this man before.

Then he remembered – it had been on the televised trial of one of the most notorious terrorists of the 1990s. Paulo had been young then, but he had noticed – and it had stuck in his mind until this moment – that the fugitive, led out of the armoured van into the court, had had a peculiar lurching gait. Paulo remembered being appalled and fascinated by the details of the man's crimes, and he never forgot his name: Sancho Pirroni – known to Interpol and to his many enemies as 'the Piranha'.

The man reached a dusty blue 4x4 and unlocked it. Paulo stood watching him, a million questions buzzing in his head. How could Sancho Pirroni be here? He was doing several life sentences in a maximum security prison in the United States. Could he be sure it was him? The Mediterranean features were hardly characteristic of Australian natives, so he certainly wasn't local. The build looked about the same as Sancho Pirroni, allowing for a little weight gain over the years. And then there was that distinctive limp.

The man was loading shopping bags onto the back seat of the car. Then he opened the driver's door. He was going to drive off. Somehow, before he did, Paulo needed get a close look at his face . . .

Amber appeared in the doorway of the shop, flexing her new boots one at a time. Paulo took her arm and whispered in her ear, 'Amber, can you make that man get out of his jeep and walk about a bit?'

Amber picked up at once on the urgency in Paulo's voice. Alpha Force were used to kidding around with each other but they also knew when a situation was deadly serious. She went into action immediately; she could ask questions later. She strolled up to the man, who was in the driver's seat, about to shut the door.

'Excuse me,' called Amber. She said it with a twang, drawing out her American accent to make it sound like she was from the deep South. A good friend of Amber's – a sophisticated young lady with wealthy parents who ran a genotech company – lived in Mississippi, and was constantly saying how people who didn't know her tended to assume because of her accent that she was some kind of simple hillbilly. Right now it suited Amber's purposes to sound uncomplicated and homespun. She silently apologized to her friend and called to the man a second time.

The man looked up and saw the slim, attractive black girl running lightly towards him. Paulo, watching from the front of the store, saw the man's eyes narrow. But that could mean nothing – it was be the natural reaction of anyone accosted by a stranger.

'So sorry to bother you,' said Amber with a drawl, 'but I wonder – could you help me? I think my tyre might be a bit flat. Could y'all come and tell me if it's OK?' She knew she could pass for a few years older than her actual age.

The man frowned, as though weighing Amber up for a moment, then removed his keys from the ignition and stepped out of the car. 'Yes, of course,' he said, and smiled at her. It was a charming smile and he spoke with an Australian accent, but there was a flavour of something else that made him sound foreign.

Amber thought quickly. A red Toyota parked on the opposite side of the yard looked a good candidate. It wasn't visible from the shop and it had only recently arrived, which meant the owners weren't likely to come out again for a few minutes. And she needed to pass Paulo to get there.

Paulo stood back in the shadows of the porch so that the direction of his gaze couldn't be seen as they went past. He watched the man intently, noting facial features as well as the uneven walk and committing them to memory. Using Hex's laptop, he could compare them with details of the real Sancho Pirroni. Just in case the man noticed him, Paulo gave Amber a soft wolf whistle as she walked by.

'You have an admirer,' the man said to Amber.

'Not my type,' she replied.

'He was watching you as you came over.'

Amber realized what was odd about the way the man spoke. There was a slight formality, as though

English wasn't his first language. It reminded her of Paulo, who would babble ten to the dozen in his native Spanish but, although fluent in English, always seemed to have trouble contracting everyday expressions. She made a mental note – details like this might be useful. There was something else she noticed too: a patch of skin on the man's left forearm that showed up pink and wrinkled against his tan, like a scar from a burn.

Amber led the man to the Toyota. She indicated the back wheel on the side facing away from the shop and poked the tyre with her finger. She was about to say, 'Does this look all right to you?' when, from inside the car, a furious wailing started. A toddler had been sitting quietly in a child seat and was now obviously upset to see two strangers looming outside the window.

The man glanced at the child and then at Amber, noting the child's light blond hair and fair skin and Amber's ebony colouring. 'Surely not your sister?' he said.

Amber's mind raced. 'Gee, no, I'm the au pair,' she said, quick as a flash. 'And pardon me, sir, but she's a he,' she added, noting the cut of the clothes. She made shushing noises at the child, hoping she sounded soothing. The child redoubled his efforts and screeched all the more loudly, his face pink with outrage.

The man looked down at the tyre. 'The tyre is perfectly all right.'

Amber gave him a dazzling smile. 'Well, thank y'all so much for that – I just wanted to be sure. If you'll excuse me, I'd better calm down li'l Tommy here.'

The lame man seemed keen to get away. He nodded curtly and began to walk back to his 4x4. Amber stood by the car as though searching for her keys. Any moment now she expected the child's parents to make an appearance to find out what was causing the ruckus, and she was relieved to see that the man was no longer looking in her direction. She noticed Alex coming around the front of the car park, heading for the shop, and slipped back inside as soon as she could.

Alex passed close to the lame man. Something made them both look round at each other at the same moment. The fraction of a second when their eyes met was like a spark igniting. Alex didn't know who the man was but he felt chilled, as though he had been searched by a piercing intelligence and unmasked.

Amber and Paulo waited until the man's jeep had left the car park before they let themselves be seen talking to one another.

'So what's all the mystery?' she said.

Paulo kept his voice low, his eyes following the dusty wake left by the jeep. 'I think we have just met one of the world's most dangerous terrorists,' he said.

4

Trail of Blood

'Sancho Pirroni?' repeated Hex. 'Isn't he in jail?' His fingers were already flying over the keys of his state-of-the-art palmtop. The flat aerial in the lid of the tiny machine connected him with a network of communications satellites, and meant that he could surf the Net from anywhere in the world – even the depths of the rainforest.

They were back at the camp, waiting for the lighting and camera technicians to arrive for a last technical rehearsal. Alex broke out a crate of water and silently handed round bottles. They found they were constantly thirsty in the sapping jungle heat, and so it was vital to keep up their intake of fluids.

'Yes, here we are.' Hex read from the screen: '"September nineteen ninety-six: the terrorist Sancho Pirroni was today sentenced to life imprisonment by a court in Washington for the murder of a German secret agent. 'Sancho the Piranha', as he has become known, will spend the rest of his life behind bars in the maximum security wing of US Penitentiary Beaumont in Texas. The sentencing brings to an end a reign of terror that lasted for more than two decades and began with the kidnapping and murder of the UN diplomat Charles Bowler. Pirroni has masterminded bombings, assassinations and kidnappings for innumerable terrorist and guerrilla groups. His employers include the Grey Wolves, who were behind the attempted assassination of Pope John Paul the Second, the Guatemalan Committee for Patriotic Unity, the Indian separatist group Harakat ul-Ansar, the Lebanese Shiite group Hezbollah, the Italian Red Brigade and the Palestine Liberation Organization. He is also reported to have worked for Saddam Hussein and Fidel Castro. Handing down the sentence, Judge Daniel Kramer said: 'You are a cold, calculating killer with no regard for human life. You will never be set free.'"'

'That's one hell of a resumé,' said Li dryly.

Paulo was frowning. 'But I saw him today. He's here.'

Amber took a slug of water. 'Hex, can you find a photo of him?'

Hex's fingers rattled the small keyboard. 'Coming right up. Hold on, I'll enhance it.' He hit a key and then handed the little machine to Amber.

The picture was blurred, an enlargement from one of the few shots taken during the televised coverage of Sancho Pirroni's trial. The angle wasn't ideal either. Half the prisoner's face was in shadow. He also looked slimmer than the man Amber had been talking to in the car park, but she tried to ignore that. She concentrated on the central features – the shape of the eyes, nose and mouth – and imagined them superimposed on the face she had seen that morning.

Li was watching Amber intently. 'You think it's him, don't you?'

Amber shrugged and handed the palmtop back to Hex. 'I can't be sure.'

'Maybe I can find something else . . .' Micro-expressions flickered over Hex's face as he checked other websites and rejected them. 'No, that seems to be the same image . . . same again . . .' He looked up. 'All the photos seem to be variations of that one. Obviously very few were taken.'

'I suppose if you were an international terrorist you wouldn't have had your photo taken that often either,' said Li.

Alex drained his water bottle and crushed it for the recycling bin. They were meticulously careful about rubbish – for two reasons. Not only were they eager to keep the rainforest free of litter, they knew that any food scraps or wrappers would attract unwanted guests such as rats. And once rats came into the camp, there would be snakes too. But Alpha Force were used to the discipline of making sure they left no trace in a camp – it could be vital on covert missions.

'There's usually an arrest photo,' said Alex. 'That must be up on a site somewhere. You know, the standard mug shot with the lines in the background that show how tall he is.'

They heard the sound of footsteps in the undergrowth. Tracey, the production executive, appeared. 'Has one of you guys got a mobile phone? Something's interfering with our equipment.' She sounded cross.

'It's my palmtop – sorry,' said Hex.

'Well will you turn it off, please?'

'E-mail my uncle before you do,' hissed Amber.

'Just what I was thinking,' replied Hex in a low voice, his fingers working like lightning. In a moment it was done. 'All switched off now,' he said brightly to Tracey.

'It shouldn't be here in the first place,' said Tracey. She spoke into her radio microphone. 'Pam, is that any better?'

The reply came from a tiny speaker on a pendant, like the remote earpiece for a mobile phone: 'We're still getting fizz on some of the cameras.'

Tracey sighed. 'Can you tell which ones?'

'It's right where you are, Tracey.'

'Well, it's not me,' she retorted. She looked around at the others. 'Right, what else have you got?'

Li, Hex, Amber, Paulo and Alex all looked at each other, mystified.

'Nothing,' protested Hex. 'Oh, wait a moment.' He looked at his watch. 'Ah yes, it was me.' He clicked a button on the watch. 'Is that better?'

'Gadget boy,' said Amber, rolling her eyes. 'Of course it would have to be you!'

Tracey spoke into her microphone again. 'How about now?'

'Much better, Tracey, thanks.'

Paulo was peering at Hex's watch. 'That's new, isn't it? What does it do?'

'It continually checks by radio with the signal for the atomic clocks in Switzerland,' said Hex. 'That way I know it's accurate.'

'Surely it's not likely to get out of sync that easily,' said Li.

'No, but I like to know it's checking,' rejoined Hex defensively. 'What's the point of having a watch if it isn't a hundred per cent accurate?'

'Yeah – goddamn, those milliseconds can slip away if you don't keep an eye on them,' said Amber sarcastically.

'Right,' said Tracey. 'What we need to do now is check out the camera blind spots so that we know our contestants can't hide from us. You've got thirty seconds to try to make yourselves invisible before we turn the cameras on. So scoot – off you go.' Her expression was still annoyed and her manner brusque.

'No peeking now,' said Li, springing to her feet.

'A camera's blind spot depends on its arc of movement and the size of its lens,' said Hex. 'I can work them out for you and plot them on a map quicker than we can test them.'

Amber clapped him on the back. 'But that wouldn't be any fun, would it? Get your lazy butt moving, Hex.'

When the cameras powered up thirty seconds later, Alpha Force were nowhere in sight.

The technical rehearsal took a couple of hours and continued after nightfall, with a pause for the animal chorus at dusk, so that the lighting could be checked and the infra-red cameras calibrated. Thanks to Alpha Force's ingenuity, by the time the camera crew finished there wasn't a nook or cranny that was not covered by at least one camera and microphone.

Finally the crew finished for the day, the fire was lit and Li and Alex did a sweep of their camp, making sure there were no snakes in any of their equipment or in the cooking pots.

As soon as the cameras were switched off for the night, Hex powered up his palmtop and connected to the Net – as he had been itching to do for the last few hours. They could also discuss the encounter with the man in the car park that morning.

Li asked, 'What makes his walk so special that you could recognize him by it?'

'Oh, it's just a cowboy thing, you know?' replied Paulo. He sat back and tipped his bush hat forwards over his nose like a Wild West hero.

'You can recognize anybody by their walk,' said Alex. 'My dad says you can change almost anything about your appearance, but the way you walk is the hardest thing to disguise.'

Li leaped to her feet. 'You're right, Alex. In fact, let me show you. You see, you've got these long gangly arms and legs, so your walk's a little bit of a swagger and a little bit of a stumble. Like a pirate crossed with a gorilla . . .'

She began to stride to and fro, taking slow steps and hunching her shoulders to exaggerate the swing of her arms. Amber clutched her sides, laughing, and Paulo lifted the hat off his face to look.

'That's not how I walk,' protested Alex.

Paulo got to his feet. 'This is how Amber walks,' he said. Setting his hat at a jaunty angle on the side of his head, he minced slowly across the camp, swaying his hips languidly. 'It's a little bit rich, a little bit gorgeous— Ow!' His performance was brought to an abrupt end as Amber threw her remaining old boot at him.

'Knew that would come in handy,' she said, dusting down her hands.

'Hey, guys,' called Hex, 'we've got mail!'

Paulo put his hat back on properly and peered over Hex's shoulder. 'Maybe it's from your uncle, Amber.'

'He's going to tell you off for dissing me,' rejoined Amber. 'He has eyes and ears everywhere.'

'Er, no,' said Hex, addressing them all. 'Actually it's for Alex.' He handed the palmtop to Alex. 'Sorry, I was in such a hurry I opened it by mistake.'

Something in Hex's tone brought a frown to Alex's face. He took the palmtop and read the message on its tiny screen.

It was from his father.

—

The army replied today. Sorry, son, it's bad news. They won't be asking you to join. Don't be too disappointed. Enjoy your holiday and we'll worry about the future later. There are plenty of other places where your ugly mug will fit just fine.

'Everything OK, Alex?' said Amber.

Stunned, Alex handed her the palmtop. Amber read it, puzzled, and her mouth fell open in surprise. She handed the palmtop on to Paulo. Each read the e-mail in turn. They didn't know what to say. They all knew that Alex had had his hopes pinned on getting into the army, following in his father's footsteps. All of them had assumed he would.

Hex sat down next to Alex and clapped him on the shoulder. 'I thought you were dead certain to get in.'

'They must be absolutely crazy,' said Amber.

'It has got to be some kind of mistake . . .' ventured Paulo.

Alex gradually tuned back into the moment. The palmtop was back in Hex's hands, the message still on the screen. Alex looked at it. Those few words had turned all his plans upside down and erased his dreams. For years he had seen his future so clearly. Now he couldn't see it at all. He felt disorientated, unreal. 'It's no mistake,' he said. He reached over and pressed the delete key.

The palmtop pinged as another e-mail arrived, this time from Amber's uncle. Hex read it out, figuring that business as usual was the best cure for the sombre mood: '"Thanks for the message, guys, but I believe it's a case of mistaken identity. I called my contacts and Sancho Pirroni is still safely behind bars. No need for heroics. Goodnight, don't let the creepy crawlies bite – and stay out of trouble! John Middleton."'

'I suppose it's highly unlikely we saw him if he's in a maximum security jail,' said Hex.

'I'm a bit disappointed, actually,' said Li. 'Hex, can't you program that machine of yours to receive only good news?' She winked at Alex but he didn't seem to notice.

'Disappointed?' echoed Amber. Her tone was incredulous. 'Surely it's a good thing that a man like that is safely behind bars!'

'Forget it,' said Li quietly. She had made the remark in an attempt to cheer Alex up, but it had come out wrong.

Paulo was shaking his head. 'I am still sure of what I saw,' he said. 'Seeing that man today was like a picture from the past.'

Alex spoke up. 'Well, I'm with Paulo.' He turned to the Argentinian. 'You're not the kind of guy who would say something if you weren't certain of it. Whoever is in that prison in the US, it isn't Sancho Pirroni.'

5

A Tiger by the Tail

It was morning, time for Alpha Force to leave. By lunch time six teenagers, the children of assorted celebrities, would be arriving at the camp which would be their home for seven days as they coped with rainforest wildlife and jungle games – and each other – in front of the TV cameras.

Alpha Force worked in silence, tidying their camp and removing all trace that they had been there. Sleeping out in the rainforest wasn't everyone's idea of five-star comfort, but none of them would have swapped it for the best hotel. The air was already humid but still just pleasantly warm – not yet the drenching heat of midday.

Li rolled up her sleeping bag and stood with her face turned to the sky. Far above in the canopy, a striped possum performed a spectacular leap from the high branches. Its body and tail were silhouetted in a graceful shape against the sunlight as it stretched through the air, then it landed with a crash in the fan palms below the high canopy.

'I'm sorry we're leaving,' said Li. 'Thanks, Amber, for getting us this gig.'

The hotel had sent a car to pick them up. As they settled into the seats, the air conditioning washed over them like ice water. They left the lush green twilight of the rainforest and headed out through diamond-hard sunlight along the coast road.

After a little while they drove round a bend and the driver slowed. The road had been empty, but here it was blocked by a queue of traffic.

'I wasn't expecting a rush hour out here in the boondocks,' said Li.

Paulo was the first to recognize where they were. 'Hey, is this the same place we came yesterday?'

'That little store?' said Amber. She peered out of the window. 'Yes, there it is.' She pointed to the shop, which was just visible between two parked lorries.

The previous day it had been a quiet coastal road with a petrol station and a shop. Today, the outside world had arrived in force. Location vans as large as removal lorries carried TV equipment and catering facilities. A couple of limousines were on hand, presumably for the presenters of the show. There was even a first-aid truck. And all needing petrol. The queue stretched out of the forecourt and into the road.

'Looks like the circus has come to town,' said Alex.

On the other side of the road a mobile news crew was setting up. A technician was hoisting a shoulder-mounted camera into position and a sound man was adjusting a boom microphone. Their equipment was plastered with the logo of the game show company. A journalist did a brief speech to camera with the line of vehicles in the background.

Hex pointed at them, incredulous. 'Are they actually filming a queue at a petrol station? Does nothing ever happen here?'

'First time I've ever seen a queue out here, that's for sure,' said their driver. He pulled in and joined the back of the line. 'Long as we're held up by this lot anyway, I might as well fill the tank. You never know when you're going to see a roadhouse, and you don't want to run out in the middle of nowhere.'

'Someone else is prudently filling up too,' said Amber. She looked pointedly at a jeep parked at one of the pumps. The owner was not in sight.

The others followed her gaze. 'Is that our friend from yesterday?' said Hex.

'Sure looks like his car,' said Amber.

The camera crew had moved to the forecourt of the petrol station and the journalist was scanning the customers paying at the kiosk. She seemed to be looking for interviewees. A figure came through the automatic doors. He had a slight but distinctive limp.

Paulo's eyes narrowed. He leaned forwards to get a better view. 'Go on, interview him,' he said quietly.

To his astonishment the journalist stepped forward and stopped the man.

Hex started to speak but Paulo and Alex waved at him to keep quiet. As one, Alpha Force held their breath. They watched the scene in silent tableau.

The journalist spoke a few words into her microphone before holding it out to the man for his reply. The man hesitated.

Paulo nodded to himself. He dared the man to reply.

The man smiled at the journalist and began to speak. From inside the car, none of their conversation could be heard, but it looked quite normal and friendly. The journalist was smiling; even the man seemed to be smiling. He talked to her for about a minute, then they seemed to part cordially and he walked awkwardly back to his car.

'She's just had a tiger by the tail,' said Paulo quietly. He exchanged a glance with Alex.

'A piranha,' corrected Alex softly.

'Leave it out, you two,' said Amber. She peered at the parked jeep. 'Anyway, he's brought his girlfriend or wife or something. Hardly what you'd expect of a terrorist in hiding.'

Ignoring the scorn dripping from Amber's voice, Alex and Paulo watched the jeep as the passenger door opened and a blonde woman climbed out.

'His girlfriend,' hissed Paulo. 'What's she up to?'

The man started the engine and manoeuvred out of the forecourt and away up the road.

'He's leaving her,' said Li. 'I wonder why?'

'Lovers' tiff?' said Amber.

'She's talking to the reporter,' said Hex.

The cameraman adjusted the focus to get her in the picture but the woman held her hand up to block his view.

'The lady is camera shy,' said Paulo.

The reporter was shaking her head at the woman. The cameraman lowered his equipment with a shrug and the sound man walked away. Obviously the conversation wasn't for public consumption.

'She looks quite upset,' said Li. 'Look at her body language. Her head, her arms . . .' The woman had her head on one side as though she was pleading, and was gesticulating with her hands. Finally she lifted her arms in a gesture of exasperation and turned on her heel. She marched across the forecourt and broke into a run, heading away along the road.

'That looks to me like a very unhappy woman,' said Hex.

'I'd say she was very frightened,' said Alex.

6
The Mask

The face of the lame man filled the screen. He looked genial and was smiling at the reporter.

'It's a bit of a surprise for us all,' he said. His slight foreignness came through in the careful way he spoke.

'And how do you feel about Daintree being the centre of attention for a few days?'

'It will be hard to get used to. Usually it is very quiet around here.'

Alex was surrounded by bustle but his full concentration was directed at the screen in front of him. Alpha Force had been invited into the production suite at the TV station's local office near the hotel to watch the day's footage being edited. An hour-long programme would show antics from the camp, cut together with interviews where the contestants, their parents, the presenters and local people talked about what they expected. A bank of screens showed different views of the camp. They flipped between the first of the teenage contestants, who were now exploring their new home. They seemed to have forgotten all about the cameras that were catching their every action to broadcast to ten million viewers in Australia and the UK.

Sequences were being run backwards and forwards as they were copied onto a master tape. Alex had watched the interview with the lame man a couple of times, and each time something about it bothered him. He racked his brain for the detail that was nagging at him.

The reporter's to-camera piece was being spliced in after the lame man's interview. 'So there we are. Residents of the Daintree area are braced for a week of notoriety as the children of some rather famous people prepare to make the jungle their home . . .'

The editor cued up some shots of the contestants. He ran through the tape backwards at high speed until he found a close-up of a face and copied it onto another tape for use in a montage. Then he looked for another.

'It's funny to be looking at it from here,' said Li.

'I'm glad I'm not being filmed,' said Hex. 'Look at that guy.'

A fat kid was sitting on one of the camp beds, fanning himself with his bush hat. He'd only been in the camp a few hours and already he looked thoroughly fed up.

'That's Peter Bailey, son of the former middleweight boxer Bill Bailey,' said the producer, a square-built woman with a grey T-shirt bearing the TV company logo. The screens around her were reflected like postage stamps in her small glasses.

'His dad's a middleweight but he's a heavyweight,' said Hex. 'There's a turn-up for the books.'

The producer clicked the mouse and a good-looking girl with two blonde plaits appeared on the screen. 'That's Milla Davey, daughter of Debbie Lynn Davey—'

'Who's she?' said Li.

'Soap star,' said the producer. 'It's strictly C-list celebs.' She clicked to another contestant, who was polishing her glasses on her T-shirt. 'Holly Ferrian, daughter of McKenzie Ferrian, the rock singer.' The producer clicked again. 'And that's Mark Roland, son of the athlete Rocket Roland.'

Mark Roland was lifting a billycan of water onto the fire, the muscles in his golden tanned arms taut with effort.

'He's rather nice,' said Amber.

On the screen, the handle of the billycan gave way and the contents splashed all over Mark. The producer gasped. 'I hope that wasn't hot.'

Mark was shaking a soaked trouser leg and grinning at the others goofily.

'No, just wet!' said Amber.

'Good. We don't want them killing themselves or being carted off to hospital with multiple burns.'

'When's the first programme due for transmission?' asked Alex.

The producer was busy making notes on a chart. The editor looked up. 'This evening,' he said. He was cursoring through some footage at double speed as he spoke. 'We're still waiting for some contestants to get out to the camp.'

Alex turned to the others. 'We'd better make sure we're back at the hotel so that we can see the show properly,' he said.

'We don't need to wait until this evening,' said Hex. They were back at the hotel and had crowded into his room. 'I took a feed from the mixing desk.' He was calling up the programme on his palmtop.

'If the producer knew . . .' said Paulo, shaking his head. 'You're a brave man to risk her wrath.'

There was some background material on the camp and then the TV reporter's spiel started. Next would come the interview with the lame man. 'Stop it there,' said Alex, just at the point where he knew the interview with the lame man had been edited in. 'Can you play it very slowly?'

He and Paulo leaned down to squint at the tiny screen. Alex turned to Paulo. 'There it is. Right at the beginning, when the reporter first approached him.'

'What?' said Amber.

'Watch,' said Alex. He clicked the cursor a few times and handed the palmtop to Amber. On the screen, there was a long shot of the petrol station that morning, and then the view switched to the face of the lame man.

Amber was shocked at what she saw. When she had talked to him in the car park, he'd struck her as friendly and charming. But the expression she saw on his features now was quite different from the images that had been playing in her peripheral vision while they were being edited. Slowed down, his first reaction to the reporter was blazing anger, like a furnace door being opened. Then it was swiftly brought under control and the normal, charming, slightly foreign resident of Daintree resurfaced.

Silently, she handed the palmtop to Hex. He watched it and passed it to Li.

When they had all seen it, Alex spoke. 'He's very controlled, very convincing. But you can't hide your micro-expressions. They're emotions that show on your face even before you're aware of them. When your auntie gives you patterned socks for Christmas, you pretend they're just what you wanted, but for a split second there'll be a curl of the lip or something that says the opposite. Only these expressions are normally too fast to see.'

'I see I'm going to have to get you a different Christmas present,' said Li.

Alex had the bit between his teeth now. He ignored Li's quip. 'This man was furious at being caught on TV. But then he decided he'd better make the best of it.'

'Lots of people don't like being photographed,' said Hex. 'What does that prove?'

'Very little, at this stage,' said Paulo. 'Hex, could we do another search on Sancho Pirroni? Let's see what we can find out.'

7

Waking the Devil

Sancho Pirroni was watching the TV. He was sitting on a wooden stool at a breakfast bar in a small kitchen. A half-door stood open to the back yard, letting in afternoon sunlight that bathed the pine units in a honey glow. Sensing the day's fiercest heat was now past, the crickets were ticking in the shrubs around the house. In all respects it seemed like a tranquil afternoon in an ordinary dwelling at the edge of the Daintree Rainforest.

Heather, his girlfriend, walked in from the yard, shopping bags in each hand. 'Hi, Peter,' she called cheerily. 'Peter' was the name Heather knew him by, like the other locals. She had no inkling of his past, though she did know he wasn't the kind of man who liked to be crossed.

Pirroni spoke without looking at her. 'Where's the tape?'

Heather had been dreading this moment. She didn't know why she had been sent to get the tape, or how her boyfriend had expected her to do it, but she was absolutely clear about one thing: failure was not an option. Yet she had failed. She had walked around crying for a while and had then called in on a friend. After a few hours of chatting and shopping she started to think it might all somehow blow over, and by the time she stepped out of the taxi with her bags she felt a lot better. But when Pirroni asked that question it was as if icy fingers had gripped her heart.

'I couldn't get it, darling,' she said quickly. She didn't dare look at him, so she busied herself packing away the shopping. 'Short of mugging the journalist, what could I do? She wasn't letting it go. Anyway, I thought you wouldn't want to attract attention. How would it have looked if I'd done something silly?'

Heather realized she was talking too fast. She forced herself to slow down: 'The programme's tonight. Maybe they won't show your bit. Or we could have another go. It'll probably be all right anyway. I'm sure I can get it later.'

Pirroni didn't look at her. His expression was blank. That made it easier for Heather to look at him. She wished she hadn't. From where she stood at the worktop, she now saw that, tucked into his waistband, was a pistol.

Heather took three deep breaths and then moved to the bread bin. 'I was going to make some bruschetta. What would you like on it?' She spoke brightly. Doing something domestic made her feel she could restore normality. She hoped he would play along.

Pirroni was silent for a moment. Then he said, 'No, I don't fancy bruschetta. In the larder there's a margarine tub, though, with a snack in it. I'll have that.'

Heather looked at the shelves and saw a small

plastic container. She pulled it out. 'It feels empty,' she said, weighing the tub in her hand.

She realized that Pirroni had got up and moved across the room. She peeked around the larder door and saw him pick up the phone and pull out its aerial.

'Who are you phoning, darling?'

'The flying doctor.'

'Are you feeling ill? Do you need the number?' Anxiety was making her gush, try to be over-helpful. She told herself to shut up.

'I've got the number,' said Pirroni, tapping on the keypad. He entered the number but did not press dial. 'Now, why don't go ahead and fetch me that snack.'

Heather started to relax. She even managed a smile. 'Sorry about the tape, darling,' she said.

'Yeah,' Pirroni said.

Heather peeled the lid off the box.

She found herself looking at a large black spider. Its body was longer than her finger, and it had a hard, glossy carapace. To her horror it reared up on its hind legs. She screamed and tried to fling the tub away from her.

The spider moved like lightning. Its long fangs made contact with her finger and sank in through the nail. Heather immediately felt a pain searing through her finger and up her arm. She tried to jerk away, to shake the spider off, but it clung fast, gripping her finger, repeatedly injecting pulses of venom as it bit and bit again.

'Help! Help me!' she screamed.

Pirroni stood looking at her, his eyes cold. He glanced at his watch.

Finally the spider let go. Pirroni studied Heather with detached interest, as though examining a specimen in a lab. Heather's eyes bulged. She was still on her feet, but she was gasping, and her face was slick with sweat. Dark patches of perspiration had collected under her arms, staining the pale-brown fabric of her shirt. Tears poured from her eyes and she clutched at her chest with her left hand. Her face started to twitch.

Pirroni glanced at his watch again, then pressed the phone's dial button. 'Yes . . . hello,' he said in a calm voice. 'I need an air ambulance right away. My girlfriend has been bitten by a spider.'

There was a pause as the voice on the other end

asked him some questions, then he spoke again. 'Symptoms? She's twitching – yes, quite badly. Yes, all over. She's salivating a lot and crying. And I think she's finding it hard to breathe.'

The doctor asked for some more information. Calmly Pirroni gave him directions to find the house. He kept one eye on Heather all the time. While he was talking she had collapsed onto the floor and begun twitching violently, her face contorting as though electric shocks were travelling under the skin. Her intercostal muscles were spasming, causing her lungs to fill with fluid. She gave a guttural cry and began to vomit.

'You're coming right away, are you?' said Pirroni down the phone.

The spider skittered across the worktop and dropped onto the floor. It came towards Pirroni. He stepped forward and trod on it firmly. Heather, slumped on the floor by the breakfast bar, her face grey, was barely aware of it.

Pirroni spoke a few more words into the phone and then cut the connection. He took the pistol out of his waistband and sat down to wait.

The doctor landed his helicopter in front of the house and was walking through the door within less than fifteen minutes. He was a confident figure in the distinctive grey overalls bearing the flying doctor emblem. He put his medical bag on the floor beside Heather's still body, and saw the dead spider where Pirroni had squashed it.

'Looks like a Sydney funnel-web,' he said, and squatted down. 'A male as well, I reckon. Nasty.' He opened Heather's left eye and peered at the pupil. 'It's good you got the spider, so we know what anti-venom to give. Although there aren't many as bad as this. We're going to need to take her in. We're a bit low on fuel because I rushed straight here from another call, but don't worry, I've got enough to get her to the hospital.' He took a needle out of a sterile wrapper and located the vein in the crook of Heather's arm. 'It's only ten kilometres.'

Pirroni considered his options. He had planned to take the helicopter and get as far away from Daintree as possible before the tape was shown and he was at risk of exposure. But he couldn't do that on ten kilometres worth of fuel. Still, the flying doctor would have his uses.

Pirroni took the pistol out of his waistband and hid it in the armchair. He got up and squatted down next to Heather.

'We'll get her right,' said the doctor. He inserted the needle in Heather's vein and fixed it with surgical tape. Then he attached a short tube to the needle and hooked that tube to a longer, flexible one attached to a bottle of saline. One side of the tube was sealed with rubber to allow drugs to be mixed in with the saline going into Heather's vein. The doctor took an ampoule from his bag.

'What's in that?' said Pirroni.

'Anti-venom,' said the doctor. 'In the old days there wasn't much we could do, but if we give this to her and get her to hospital she should be fine.' He took a sealed syringe from his medical bag and tore off its wrapper.

'Is it powerful?' said Pirroni.

'Too right it is,' said the doctor. Using the hypodermic needle he pierced the rubber seal on the ampoule and drew up the liquid into the body of the syringe. 'You wouldn't want to be given this if you weren't sure what spider it was. The wrong anti-venom is as bad as the bite itself.'

'Could it kill you?'

'Definitely. Even though she's in a bad way, I have to give the first dose slowly through a drip as she could have a bad reaction.'

Pirroni moved closer to Heather. He put his hand to her forehead and frowned with feigned concern. As the doctor started to inject the anti-venom into the saline drip, Pirroni pulled Heather's arm away violently. The doctor fell forwards. Pirroni grabbed his wrist. With his other hand he grasped the syringe, levered it out of the doctor's fingers and jabbed it into the doctor's thigh, ramming the plunger down.

The doctor yelled and struggled. Pirroni discarded the spent syringe and caught both his wrists, leaning over to pin him to the ground with his weight. The doctor's face began to turn blotchy; he gulped for breath. He tried to knee Pirroni in the ribs, but the kicks were weak and Pirroni ignored them. A hoarse, rasping sound came from deep in his throat and

Pirroni could see through his open mouth that his tongue was becoming fat and swollen. Pirroni continued to hold him down and felt the strength drain out of him as his airway narrowed and then closed.

After ten minutes Pirroni was satisfied that the doctor had stopped breathing. He released his hold and went to sit in the armchair. He picked up the pistol, just in case. Then he checked his watch and settled down to wait. The doctor's heart would stop soon. Pirroni turned his attention to Heather, who lay on her back where Pirroni had left her, mouth gaping. Her chest was no longer heaving and she had stopped making the desperate gasping noise as she tried to drag air into her lungs. Her eyes were open, but they were still and dull, like pebbles.

Presently, Pirroni got up, took hold of the doctor's arm and pulled him onto his back. The man's eyes stared up. Pirroni checked for a pulse. Nothing. He manhandled the corpse into a sitting position and began to unbutton the flying doctor's suit.

A few minutes later Pirroni emerged from the house wearing the flying doctor uniform. The helicopter was in the drive. Its grey livery and emblem mirrored the colours of the uniform. Too bad it didn't have enough fuel to get clean away. Pirroni ignored it and went towards his jeep, tossing into the back the doctor's bag and a large, heavy holdall. He had a back-up plan.

8

Wolf in Sheep's Clothing

Hex, perched on the end of the bed in his hotel room, was working his computer magic. The others sat in a semicircle on the floor in front of him, waiting. A selection of websites were at Hex's fingertips. He was the digital shaman, able to unlock secrets with the computer codes at his disposal.

He scanned through the sites he'd found, his expression grim. 'I do hope that isn't Pirroni,' he said. 'If it is, he certainly won't be happy that he's been found. And he looks like real trouble.'

Hex continued to flick through the websites. 'All the stuff we've seen before . . .' He clicked through more links. 'Oh – here's something new. MI5 set up an ambush for him at a flat in London. They thought they'd got him when he was visiting some student. Four armed police were sent to arrest him. The student let them in and the police told Pirroni to put his hands up. Instead he got his gun and killed all four of them before they could fire a single shot at him. Every bullet between the eyes.'

Amber whistled softly.

Hex was still tapping away. 'Hmm . . . This is good. Visible distinguishing marks . . . Oh.' Hex looked at the screen, surprised. 'He's got a tattoo on his left forearm. Did our man have a tattoo?'

Alex looked at Amber. 'Amber, did you see anything?'

Amber racked her brains. 'No, I don't think so. I'd have noticed something as obvious as a tattoo,' she mused. 'Wait a minute – he had a scar, like a burn—'

Li finished the sentence for her. 'Like he had had a tattoo removed?'

Amber nodded. 'Could be.'

Hex rattled over the keys again. 'I've found another picture. This is a bit naughty, but it might be interesting.'

'Er . . . a bit naughty?' said Amber. 'In what way?'

'It's a secure website.' Hex was more interested in the protocols of hacking than in batting double entendres back and forth. 'Hopefully it's the police arrest photo.' The screen flashed up a picture. Hex looked at it closely. 'Yeah,' he said after a moment. 'This is better than the other one. It's full face.' He swore under his breath.

'What is it, Hex?' said Alex. Hex handed him the palmtop. Alex looked at the picture. To the others watching him his expression was unreadable. He handed the palmtop to Paulo.

Paulo looked at the picture. He nodded very slowly to himself.

'Nice catch, Paulo,' said Alex quietly.

Paulo passed the palmtop on. Li and Amber looked at the picture in silence. Amber felt a shiver run down her spine. This time there was no mistaking it: the face in the picture was definitely the man they had seen in the car park the day before.

When it got back to Hex, he began typing again. 'Might as well be hanged for a sheep as a lamb. Let's see who's in US Penitentiary Beaumont in Texas.' The screen bleeped a few times. 'Ah,' said Hex, 'you think you can keep me out with a few passwords?' He flipped into another window and accessed another website.

Hex, like all expert hackers, had developed some powerful software tools, but to save space on his own machine he had hidden them away on servers all over the World Wide Web. When he developed or updated a tool, perhaps for encryption, decryption or password cracking, he would hack into a site, assess the level of security and hide the program in a secret passworded area only he could access. So adept was Hex at covering his tracks that the owners of these servers had no idea they were hosting software that belonged to an outsider. The advantage to Hex was that instead of carrying around dozens of programs and updating them regularly, he only had to store the addresses.

He typed in a barrage of commands and waited. ‘Here it comes,’ he said in a low voice.

Paulo was watching Hex’s expression closely. ‘What have you found, Hex?’

But Hex was already on his feet. ‘The screen’s too small to say for sure. I’ll see if I can get some larger hard copies.’ He was out of the door before anyone could say anything.

‘How’s he going to do that?’ wondered Amber.

After five minutes Hex came back with two sheets of A4 paper. ‘I spoke sweetly to one of the girls at reception and explained I needed some printouts.’ He handed one to Paulo. ‘This one’s the arrest photo.’ He passed over the second one. ‘And this one is from the prison in Texas.’

Paulo put the two pictures on the table and looked at them in silence. Hex had blown each of them up so that it filled an entire sheet. The faces were similar, with the same Mediterranean eyes and upturned mouth. Superficially, they could be the same person. But having seen the man in the flesh made all the difference. To Paulo, the prison photo looked like a different person, but he couldn’t say exactly why. The man in the arrest photo looked detached and cold. The man in the prison photo had an expression of keenness. But surely it had to be more than just a question of mood.

Li, seeming to read his mind, put her finger on the crucial detail. 'One of them may have been made to look like the other by plastic surgery. But the man in jail in Texas uses his face in a different way from the man in the arrest photo. You can see by the lines around his eyes and mouth, the way he habitually smiles or frowns. They are different people.'

Amber shuddered as her encounter with the man in the car park came back to her. 'That means Sancho Pirroni got someone to take his place when he went to jail.'

Hex's fingers pounded the keys like machine-gun fire. 'I think it's time to e-mail all this to a few people,' he said.

Pirroni took the road into the rainforest. He drove fast, and made the two-hour drive in one and a half hours. He knew he had reached his destination when he came to the convoy of trucks. The vehicles that had been queuing at the tiny petrol station were now standing in a line beside the road.

A thickset man in a security guard uniform peered into the car. Pirroni reached for the flying doctor's hat lying on the passenger seat beside him and showed the badge to the guard. The guard stepped aside and waved him on.

Pirroni found a place to park and cut the engine. He put on the hat and checked in the jeep's rearview mirror that it was pulled well down. He hefted his heavy holdall out of the back seat and over one shoulder, then took his doctor's bag and slammed the door shut. He looked around for a friendly face.

A technician was walking away from the catering truck, sipping at a plastic cup of iced coffee. Pirroni went up to him. 'Which way to the tape store?' he asked.

The technician looked bemused. 'The tape store?'

'My colleague left something here when he was up earlier.'

'Has someone hurt themselves already, Doc? Jeez, that was fast going.'

'It was a health and safety check for the crew,' said Pirroni. 'My colleague loaned a videotape on snake bites – that sort of thing. I need to collect it.'

The technician was still puzzled. 'As far as I know, everything's in the one location. We're not allowed to disturb the rainforest too much, you see, on account of there's only a few million acres of it so one beer can could destroy the whole ecosystem or something. So anything your mate left here would be at the control room, I guess. Or they'll have thrown it away.'

'Which way is the control room?' said Pirroni.

The technician pointed. 'Just follow the cables, you can't go wrong.'

Thick black rubberized cables snaked out of two of the lorries and into the jungle. 'Thank you,' said Pirroni. He began to follow them. A few metres from the road they were lifted off the jungle floor on stout pegs driven into the ground, so that they formed a kind of handrail that threaded through the trees.

Already a path was being formed where personnel were constantly passing back and forth from the trucks to the control room. Here under the trees, visibility was limited. Stout tree trunks were crowded in, making it difficult to see very far ahead, and the light that filtered through from the canopy above was dim and green.

Pirroni was on his guard, looking and listening as he walked along. He heard footsteps coming towards him and stopped. A man in shorts and a big bush hat bustled past him, ticking off boxes on a clipboard. He glanced at Pirroni and nodded. 'G'day.'

'G'day,' said Pirroni in return. He watched the man go before relaxing his grip on the gun under his jacket.

Pirroni came to a couple of chemical toilets; beyond them was a large wooden structure on stilts. This must be the control room. The cables looped up into the trees, and when he followed them with his eye, he saw they were bundled together and tethered along the side of the building. Out of long habit, he stopped as soon as he had a good view and committed the features of the building to memory. Then he walked all the way around it to check it thoroughly. There was one exit – a wooden staircase. It led up to a gantry like a veranda, with a simple wooden balustrade. It was about five metres off the ground – high enough to be difficult to escape from if jumping was the only option. The trees were too far away to be used as escape routes. Looking at it from underneath he noted that it had a simple wooden floor, no trap doors. The only hole was the access point for the cabling. A window overlooked the camp, where Pirroni could see a group of people moving round a central fire.

He listened for a moment. Anyone walking about in the control room would be easily audible on the wooden planking. He heard the scrape of a chair, and then another from a different place – there was more than one person in the room. Pirroni waited a little longer but it was not possible to tell how many people were in there. As he heard no footsteps, he figured they were probably all sitting down.

He did another circuit of the building, looking up at the roof. There were no obvious hatches that could be used as entry points – none that he could see, anyway. He made a mental note to check the ceiling as soon as he got inside. But for now it looked as though the only way in or out was the one door.

Pirroni hoped he would not need any of this information. But old habits died hard. In all his adult life, he had never entered a building without making sure he knew exactly how other people could get in and how he would get out – and where he would go afterwards.

He walked to the foot of the stairs and began to climb.

Two female technicians were in the control room, plus a face Pirroni recognized: Jonny Cale, a famous TV presenter. The technicians didn't even glance up as he opened the door. They were obviously used to comings and goings all the time.

A bank of television screens filled one wall – about a dozen of them. The pictures showed different views of the jungle camp. Pirroni noted that the contestants were seated on logs around the camp fire, waiting for something to happen.

It was Jonny Cale who spoke. 'G'day, Doc. Have we killed one of them already?'

One of the technicians, who was wearing a black baseball cap, tittered softly and Jonny Cale caught her eye. The other technician concentrated steadfastly on her work.

Pirroni smiled at Jonny. 'I won't disturb you for long. I am looking for a health and safety tape. My colleague left it here earlier.'

Jonny didn't remember a health and safety tape but he never thought to question the man as he seemed so confident and certain. 'Ah, well . . . a tape,' said Jonny. 'We're up to our eyes in them. Could be anywhere.' He smiled broadly, as though he expected to get a laugh, and looked round at the two women.

Pirroni kept his voice pleasant. 'If you don't mind, I'm in a hurry.'

The technician in the black baseball cap swung her chair round. 'It's probably been put away somewhere by mistake. We're filling tapes all the time. The ones we've recorded today are in that rack there. Once we've edited them into a programme they're moved to one of the vans.'

'Thank you.' Pirroni squatted down beside the rack. There was some equipment between him and the technicians, which gave him good cover should he need it.

Jonny stood up. 'Well, I must love you and leave you, I'm afraid. Time to give this lot a briefing about the game. I'll be talking to camera three – that right?'

'Fine, Jonny,' said the technician in the baseball cap.

Jonny gave the room a dazzling smile and exited.

There were two tapes in the cupboard, both with labels that indicated they had been used that afternoon. Pirroni looked up. 'The one I need is not here.'

'Oh well, perhaps it's got mixed up among the edited tapes and gone to the van,' said the technician in the baseball cap. 'That's back the way you came, then one of the security guards will direct you. Sorry about this.'

The other technician, who had not spoken until now, looked up. 'Unless Interpol got it.'

Her colleague looked blank. 'Interpol? What are you talking about.'

'Maybe it was when you were having your break. About half an hour ago some guys from Interpol came in and said they needed to investigate some of our tapes.'

'You're kidding.'

'I swear on my signed Jonny Cale poster I am not.' Both women burst into a storm of mischievous giggles.

'No, seriously,' said the technician in the baseball cap. 'Give.'

'Well, these guys came in, flashed around a big badge with a heavy silver thing on it and said they were seizing the tapes. They didn't say why. They were armed as well – one of them had this pistol in a shoulder holster.'

'Wow. Were they good-looking?' The technician's eyes goggled. She glanced at Pirroni. 'Sorry, Doc,' she said, laughing. 'Sounds like Poirot beat you to it. Still, it does mean they'll know what to do if they get a snakebite now, I guess! Won't be quite what they were expecting . . .' Pirroni laughed too. He stood up. His priority now was to get out unobtrusively. 'Thanks for your help. I'll check at the van on my way out anyway.'

He stepped out of the cabin onto the veranda

and closed the door. As he descended the steps, slightly awkwardly because of his leg, he decided to forget about the tape and drive away. He still had the initiative and he could put a significant distance between himself and the place where he had been filmed.

He set off along the jungle path, following the looped cables. He walked at a normal speed but listened with every step he took in case someone was coming the other way. Every now and then a squawk high up in the canopy drowned out the surrounding noises, and Pirroni stood still until he could hear his surroundings again. Footsteps announced a large, heavy figure, and a moment later a tall workman in jeans appeared with a coiled cable slung over his shoulder like a lasso. Pirroni stepped aside to let him pass and then continued on his way.

A crash sounded high up in the trees as a striped possum performed one of its leaps. Several birds squawked in response. Once again, Pirroni froze until the sounds had died down.

Coming around a tree he heard the chirrup of a mobile phone. A woman's voice started to speak.

Pirroni stood stock-still behind the bole of the tree and listened.

'Interpol were here, would you believe?' the woman's voice said. 'I've been talking to them just now.' She was just metres away from him and coming closer as she spoke into the phone. It was the reporter who had accosted him at the petrol station that morning.

She was too close now for him to turn round or take any evasive action. Pirroni walked on towards her.

'They said it was someone I interviewed this morning and they were asking me for a description of him – if there was anything odd about him. Yeah, the one on the show.'

She was right in front of him, but was concentrating on the phone conversation. She registered that there was someone in front of her and turned her body to let him go by. Pirroni passed her. His mind was working furiously. If the place was crawling with Interpol agents, he might have to find somewhere to hide until they left. If they had already gone, he needed to find that out too.

Whatever, he now couldn't risk going straight back to the jeep.

He heard the reporter say, 'Hang on, I'll call you back.' Then she called after him, 'Hey, Doc – got a moment?'

Pirroni stopped.

The reporter touched him on the shoulder as he turned round. 'Sorry to disturb you, Doc. Could you just tell me if this bite's OK? It's rather sore.' She held out her hand and peered up under the rim of his hat.

Then her expression changed. She started to step back.

Pirroni knew that expression well. In a moment would come the scream. He pulled out his gun and her face changed again, the scream swallowed at the sight of this new threat. She'd gone limp with fear and it was easy for Pirroni to grab her mobile phone. He slipped it into his pocket. Then he took her by the arm and steered her off the track into the trees. She tried to resist for the first few steps, but he leaned close to her ear and said, 'Just walk. You'll be fine.' He hurried her on into the undergrowth and she stumbled. He whispered in her ear again and she began to pick up her feet carefully.

Pirroni's first thought was to find a place to dispose of her quietly. Out here in the jungle she wouldn't be found for a while. Possibly not ever. But he couldn't be sure a camera wasn't on him.

He was getting close to the main camp. There were voices, the loudest of which were the cajoling tones of Jonny Cale. Pirroni also heard a soft electric whir. He glanced up into the canopy and saw cameras on platforms fixed seven metres up in the trees. The one he was looking at moved in a slow arc. The cameras were remotely operated. That was good. It meant there'd be fewer personnel in the surrounding area.

The reporter was breathing hard. She concentrated very carefully on moving without tripping and tried not to think about anything else. In fact, she couldn't think about anything else. If she did she might make a mistake, and she did not want to give Pirroni any reason to whisper in her ear again. Anyway, they were coming to the camp. There were plenty of people there and surely that would be all right. They would be on TV. Then she could stop. Surely then he'd let her go.

Suddenly they were in the clearing and the camp was in front of them. The contestants, still sitting on their logs, all turned and stared. The presenter Jonny Cale, standing beside the fire, called out in irritation into his microphone, 'Cut! Cut, blast it. We'll have to go again. Some bozo's blundered right into the shot.'

Pirroni took hold of the reporter's arm and moved her sideways on towards the group. He lifted his pistol and put it to her head. 'If nobody moves,' he said calmly, 'nobody will get hurt.'

Pandemonium broke out. Somebody let out a strange screaming wail. Some of the contestants got to their feet and looked around wildly. Jonny Cale was attempting to call for quiet, his arms flapping, but he had no hold on the contestants' attention. They looked only at the reporter, reacted only to the terror on her face. Helplessly, they looked at each other.

Pirroni watched them for a moment. Keeping the gun visible, he took the reporter's phone out of his pocket and with one hand levered the back off. He removed the battery and threw it on the fire. It exploded with a loud bang.

There were several more screams, which quickly faded. In the silence that replaced them, seven pairs of eyes turned to stare at him. 'I've got grenades,' said Pirroni, 'and I will use them. I need you all to be very quiet, very calm and to follow my instructions.'

They looked back at him.

He put his gun to the reporter's temple. A tear rolled down her cheek. 'Now all of you stand up.'

The contestants all got to their feet.

A movement flicked the bushes at the edge of Pirroni's peripheral vision. He turned and instinct made him dive to one side, knocking over the journalist. He saw a flash and the shot followed. The gun made a hiss, not a crack. It wasn't a bullet. That explained why he had time to dodge out of the way. Pirroni recovered his balance even before the animals and birds responded. As they fled through the trees, screeching, he already had his gun lifted. He took aim carefully and squeezed the trigger. The forest echoed to the sound of his shot and a body fell heavily to the ground.

The contestants stared in horror. Some of them hid their faces when they registered the buff-coloured shirt, the bush hat rolling away, and the lolling head.

It was one of the rangers. Blood seeped from a red hole between the man's eyes.

9
Siege

It was Amber's room they knocked at first. She'd been about to go down to the pool for a swim. She opened the door to find two men in pale blue police uniforms.

One of them held up an identity card. 'Good afternoon, ma'am. Are you Amber Middleton?'

Amber nodded.

'I believe you were out at the TV studio in the Daintree Rainforest earlier today?'

Amber nodded again. 'Yes.'

'We'd appreciate it if you would come with us.'

'What's this all about? Has something happened at the camp?'

'Sorry, we can't tell you anything right now. We simply have orders to escort you out there to help us with our enquiries,' replied one of the policemen.

Amber saw that she wasn't going to get anything further out of them, so she shrugged and followed them out of the hotel.

Outside on the drive stood two white Holden Commodore saloons with the characteristic blue markings of the Queensland Police. The two officers showed Amber to one of the cars. As she climbed in, she saw Hex coming down the front steps with Alex. Li and Paulo followed close behind.

Amber shot them a questioning glance, but they shrugged back at her, obviously as much in the dark as she was.

Alex and Hex joined Amber in the first car. Li and Paulo got into the second.

'Strap yourselves in,' said the driver as he swung into the seat. 'We've got no time to waste.'

His colleague spoke into his radio. 'JN Five en route. Request backup. Over.'

The driver stopped the car at the hotel gates and checked the road. It was clear. He punched a switch on the dashboard and the siren began to wail. With one last look in each direction he floored the accelerator. The V8 engine answered. The tyres spun for a moment on the loose dust of the road, then bit. The car pulled out and roared up the carriageway.

They were fast approaching a lorry. It pulled aside for them to pass and they left it behind in a flash.

Amber, Hex and Alex turned and looked through the rear window. The other police car was close behind, nipping around the truck and swinging back into the right lane. Even traffic coming the other way was pulling to the side to get out of their way. The police drivers used the full width of the road whenever there was a corner, veering back and forth across the central white line.

Alex sneaked a look at the speedometer. It said 225 k.p.h. They passed another truck. It seemed to be crawling. Alex wanted to talk to the others to see if they knew what was going on, but conversation was impossible over the roar of the engine, the noise of the road and the wail of the siren. He glanced at his friends. Amber's eyes were dancing like points of light in her dark face. 'Lovin' this!' she mouthed with a huge grin.

Hex was staring ahead, his expression glazed and blissful, as though he was listening to a favourite piece of music very, very loud.

In the distance, Alpha Force could now see blue police lights throwing strobes into the sky. A sign for a roundabout came up. The cars slowed and slalomed through without missing a beat. Police motorcycles were positioned at the roundabout exits, blocking them off so that the cars could cruise through smoothly. Then the two Commodores were off up the straight coast road again, the 5.7 litre engines taking them effortlessly back up to top speed.

When they reached the encampment in the rain-forest, they found it surrounded by a police cordon. It was early evening and the sky above the trees was blood-red. Floodlights made the area at the road-side as bright as midday, but under the trees the green gloom was turning to purple dusk. Police cars and an ambulance were parked across the road. Blue and white police tape extended into the undergrowth. Officers were picking their way in, using the tape as a guide.

Alpha Force climbed out. Beyond the police cars they could see the location trucks standing in a line. To the ticking and chirruping of the jungle creatures was added an new voice – the tinny crackle of police radios. The five friends looked at each other in astonishment. What could have happened to turn the TV shoot into a crime scene?

Another policeman ducked under the tape. 'Here they are, chief,' said one of the drivers.

The police officer looked at him. 'What took you so long?' Then, before the driver could answer, he addressed the five youngsters. 'Would you come this way, please?'

He led them to one of the location trucks and knocked once.

A voice from inside called out, 'Yes?'

'The witnesses are here, Sergeant Powell.'

Alex, Li, Hex, Amber and Paulo all looked at each other, the same thought going through their heads. Witnesses?

'Send them in.'

Alex went up the tiny steps first and entered the truck. The others followed, along with the police officer. The entire truck had obviously been converted for use as a dressing room, perhaps for the notoriously demanding Jonny Cale. There was a table in the middle, still bearing traces of make-up, which looked as if it had been pulled away from the mirror along the far wall. Now a plan of the camp was spread out on its surface. A large sofa had been pushed aside and squashed into one corner, along with cushions and a minibar. Alex could just picture the scene: the soldiers arriving, requisitioning it as an operations room and then excluding all non-military personnel; the army operating like a well-oiled machine. A pang came over him as he remembered that this wouldn't be his future after all.

Sergeant Powell, a thickset man in army fatigues, got to his feet. Alex immediately noticed his beret. It was sand coloured, with a distinctive cap badge depicting a winged sword. It was an item as familiar as anything from Alex's own home. He wasn't close enough to read the motto furled around the blade but he knew it well: 'Who Dares Wins'. The SAS. Why were they here?

Sergeant Powell stepped forward. 'Please sit down.' He motioned towards the chairs around the table.

They sat down. The police officer remained standing in the corner, as though keeping a watchful eye on proceedings.

Sergeant Powell consulted a clipboard. 'You must be Li,' he said to the Anglo-Chinese girl. He ticked off the others. 'Amber . . . Paulo . . . That takes care of the obvious ones.' He smiled, then looked at the remaining two. 'Who's Alexander and who's Melvin?'

All eyes turned on Hex. '*Melvin?*' drawled Amber. 'Don't tell me that's your real name!'

'No,' hissed Hex. 'My real name is Hex. Melvin is just what some idiot put on my birth certificate.' He looked daggers at Amber. The others kept their eyes firmly down.

'Sorry – Hex,' said Sergeant Powell with a grin. 'The police got all your passport details. We don't get information from people without knowing who they are.' His expression became serious. 'We have a siege situation in the camp. One person has been killed and eight have been taken hostage. Six of them are minors. The hostage taker is a dangerous terrorist who was thought to be in jail in America. He's been hiding out here for years but a journalist interviewed him by chance this morning and someone tipped off Interpol. Now he's demanding safe passage to a neutral country.'

Hex and Paulo exchanged glances. Their e-mail to John Middleton had got through. He must have forwarded it to his contacts immediately.

Sergeant Powell paused to let this information sink in. 'We may need to storm the camp, so we need to get a picture of the layout. You were there earlier and I understand you also helped set up the games. So what can you tell me?'

It was Li who spoke. 'Quite a lot. We've been over most of the camp and the surrounding jungle in the past few days.'

'That's good. Anything you can tell us – absolutely anything – may be useful.' Powell rotated the map on the table so that it faced the five youngsters.

Hex picked up a pencil and looked around at the others. 'Shall we start by marking where all the cameras and microphones are?'

Alex nodded. 'That's your department, Hex.'

Hex got to work drawing. Sergeant Powell watched him with interest. These kids were focused and able to concentrate immediately, he thought, as though they were doing a job. So far everyone else he'd interviewed had been thoroughly scared.

'Who are the hostages?' Amber asked.

'He's got the contestants, the TV presenter and a journalist,' Powell told her. 'They're in the control room.'

Alex was thinking aloud. 'There's only one way in and out of the control room so he's well protected. It's small so he can keep tabs on anyone with him. And it's all made of wood so if you try to climb on the roof or up the sides he'll hear you coming.'

'I suppose he's armed,' said Li.

The police officer spoke. 'If you just stick to the

facts, miss, we'll let the soldiers put together the battle plans, shall we?'

Sergeant Powell sat back in his chair and addressed the policeman. 'Officer, any chance of getting something to drink? For my men as well; it's easy to get dehydrated in this climate. Some bottled water would be great.'

'Right, sir.' The police officer pulled open the door and left.

Paulo's face had a brooding expression. Once the policeman had gone he spoke. 'Sergeant, how did he take the hostages?'

'We're not absolutely clear. We have an eye-witness account – the technician who was in the control room. When she saw what was going down she ran for it. She was still in a state when we talked to her. But she said our man walked into the camp with a female journalist at gunpoint. He shot one man and made everyone go into the control room.'

As Sergeant Powell spoke he indicated the points on the map, on which Hex was labelling his diagrams. 'The witness only saw a handgun but we think he's quite well armed,' Powell added. 'She believed he threw a grenade into the fire.'

They all started to speak at once. Li got in first. 'He threw a grenade into the fire? You don't need a fire to detonate a grenade.'

Powell nodded. 'As I said, the witness was a bit confused. That's normal. It all happens so quickly that it doesn't always make sense. But he caused an explosion of some sort, so we have to act as though he has explosives.'

Paulo said quietly, 'Or he cleverly improvised something. Which might be worse.'

Alex caught his eye and nodded.

The sergeant agreed. 'That's right. Whatever he has or hasn't got, our man is very dangerous. He's very experienced in siege situations because he's set up a stronghold he can protect all by himself. We can't surround the camp because it's a huge area and thick jungle. He's got cameras that show him what's going on. The place was constructed so that no-one could get a view from outside the perimeter. We could send a squad in but we don't know what he can see and what he can't. If we go in and we're seen, we'll be putting lives at risk. He's already shown he is prepared to kill.'

They nodded. The area of the camp was a patch of jungle larger than a football stadium and fully wired up with sound equipment and cameras – including some with night sight. And all of it controlled now by Pirroni. It was an impregnable tactical position. A direct assault, even by crack SAS troops, would mean certain death for the hostages.

'Who did he kill?' asked Amber.

'One of the rangers took a pop at him with a tranquillizer gun, of all things. Brave, but stupid against a man like this. He's an expert shot.'

'A tranquillizer gun?' repeated Alex.

'They had it to make the crocodile game look good – I guess they decided to keep them loaded after what happened,' said Amber. She thought about the day when they had tried out the games. It seemed a long time ago now. Even escaping from a crocodile seemed like straightforward fun compared to this.

Paulo said carefully, 'I expect you know who your target is.'

Sergeant Powell nodded. 'Interpol identified him. They came by to seize the filmed material.'

Paulo and the others exchanged glances. Powell noticed, but let it pass. 'Then our target arrived. If he'd got here five minutes earlier, he'd have run straight into them. He must have a sixth sense.'

Hex finished his drawing and rotated the map back towards the sergeant. 'The cameras are all remotely operated, and co-ordinated from inside the control room. The cameras that point to the camp are on all the time.'

Sergeant Powell pointed to areas away from the camp. 'What are those?'

'The game areas,' replied Hex. 'That's the crocodile lake, that's the bungee tree – but they're filmed manually as they're not used all the time. There aren't any permanent cameras there. The only place where he's got twenty-four-hour surveillance is in the central area around the camp and the control room.'

Sergeant Powell pointed to the control room on the plan. 'Are there any cameras or microphones inside?'

Hex shook his head. 'No; they don't film in there and they don't need them. But the exit is covered by the main cameras, so he can see if there's anything outside his door.'

'And you can't set up a bug in that building without being heard,' said Alex. He spoke rapidly as his brain raced through possibilities. 'Could something on the inside be adapted?'

For a moment he and Hex forgot about the SAS man sitting in front of them. Hex replied vehemently. 'Not a chance. You can convert speakers into microphones and things like that but it takes a bit of obvious rewiring. And it's a bit amateur.'

An interested expression passed across Sergeant Powell's face as he followed the exchange, but when he spoke he kept his thoughts to himself. 'If the automatic cameras are filming the camp all the time, they'll have footage of when our man seized the hostages. It would be good to see that.'

'Well yeah, but it's all in the control room,' said Hex. 'The cameras are on a closed circuit and all feed into there. And that means our target can see everything that's going on and we can't.'

'Those cameras are our best chance,' said Sergeant Powell, emphasizing the words by stabbing with his finger on the table. 'They're a purpose-built surveillance system. They've even got light intensifiers in case the contestants are doing something interesting in the dark. The way it is right now, our man could even escape through the jungle and we wouldn't know. We'd never be able to find him in an area as big and as dense as this. We need to be able to see what's on those cameras.'

Amber spoke. 'Could we get a feed off one of them? Splice in another cable or something?'

Hex was nodding. 'Just what I was thinking.'

'The problem would be getting somebody close enough without our man spotting them on camera,' said Sergeant Powell. 'I've got snipers on standby but I can't send them in until I know what he can see and what he can't.'

'Ah,' said Li. 'At the moment the cameras are locked in place on a fixed sweep. But the producer wanted them to be adjusted for a wider arc in case one of the contestants throws a strop and escapes. They needed to be able to track the contestants at all times because someone heading out into the jungle is bound to fall over something or get lost.'

Alex said, 'We need to get somebody in there and put a line into the camera circuit before he works out how to take the lock off.'

'How do we know he has not done that already?' asked Paulo. 'It's just a matter of adjusting the cameras' field of view from the control room, after all.'

'We're going to take a calculated risk,' said Sergeant Powell. 'He hasn't got anyone technical in there. We're pretty sure that neither the presenter nor the journalist knows anything about video technology. My men have been keeping our target talking to a negotiator for the past half hour, so he's had less time to think about using the equipment he's got – or hurting anyone. Hex, how tricky is it to tap the camera circuit?'

'You'd need to splice the signal cable,' said Hex. 'Easy enough, given a minute or two with the camera and a pair of pliers.'

Sergeant Powell looked at his watch. 'We've got a technician here but she's been given sedatives for shock. She won't be any use for twelve hours.' He sighed – a harsh, exasperated sound. 'The only other person we've got is a health and safety officer who keeps telling us to be careful because the undischarged tranquillizer dart lying out there in the bushes somewhere could prick someone accidentally. We've sent a car to the cameraman's house but even if they find him he won't get here for at least another hour. I could put one of my men in but they're not experienced with these new digital TV cameras.'

Hex said, 'I'm doing electrical engineering at college. I could rig up a tap.'

'I'm sure you could,' replied Sergeant Powell. 'The question is whether I should let you.'

But Hex thought he looked as though he was considering it.

The sergeant reached into his pocket and put a small device to the table. It was a black box with a socket in one end. He slid it across to Hex. 'Tell me what that is.'

A glance was enough for Hex. 'A signal splitter. If you splice that into the output cable of one of the cameras, it will transmit what they are seeing to an external source.'

Sergeant Powell was nodding. There was no doubt Hex knew what he was talking about.

Hex looked at the soldier squarely. 'Do you have an hour to wait while a cameraman gets here? Assuming you can get hold of him in the first place?'

'It will be dark by then anyway,' said Paulo. 'We need to do this while it is still light.'

Li chipped in. 'Also, we know where the camera blind spots are because we worked them all out with the crew this morning.'

Powell was thinking, his eyes narrowed. 'Where's this camera?'

'Any will do. There's one here.' Hex swivelled the map round so that it faced him again and jabbed a point he had circled. 'It's near the road so we wouldn't even have to go very far into the jungle.'

Sergeant Powell looked grave. 'You assure me that you can do this without going anywhere near the control room?'

Alex met his gaze. 'Nowhere near.'

The SAS man pushed the signal splitter all the way across to Hex and rose to his feet. 'All right. You go in, you do it and you get out. Stay out of trouble. And say nothing. If anyone finds out I let you do this, I'm toast. I wouldn't even consider it, only there are eight lives at stake and we can't wait around sitting on our thumbs. I'd send one of my men with you, but if our target spots any obvious military action, one of the hostages might be killed and I can't risk that at this stage.'

Hex pocketed the device. They all got up and filed out of the lorry.

Alex was the last. Sergeant Powell called him back. 'Alex? Your dad's in the Regiment, isn't he?'

Alex turned back from the doorway, surprised. 'Yes,' he replied. 'Back in England.' He looked at Sergeant Powell with curiosity for a moment and then added, 'Was that in my passport too?'

Sergeant Powell gave Alex a profound look. 'It's been a pleasure to meet you.' He waved his hand. 'Now go in and get out safely.'

10
Into the Lair

As they walked away from the lorry, Alpha Force were already fine-tuning the plan.

'Hex,' said Alex, 'what's the best way to do this?'

Hex replied immediately. 'I'll be OK on my own.'

Alex didn't like the sound of that. 'Someone ought to come with you,' he said. 'To keep a lookout.' He didn't want Hex going into the jungle alone. Hex was an expert in all areas of communications, but Alex felt he had the edge when it came to survival. And Sergeant Powell's last remark had made Alex feel he was responsible.

'There's no sense in two of us going,' said Hex. 'It's just a matter of splicing some cables. I'll be fine.'

'In that case I could do it myself. I can get in and out quickly—'

Hex didn't let him finish. 'Yeah, but these digital feed cameras are not like CCTV. They've got complicated error checking. If you don't time it right you'll give the game away. It's got to be me.'

'It's better if Alex goes with you, Hex,' said Paulo. He could see Hex was annoyed. 'Look, I'm not saying you couldn't handle it. But you'll have your hands full working on the camera. Let Alex be on the lookout for anything else.'

Hex shrugged. He was still irritated. Attaching the device to a camera was a simple job – for him at least – and he felt Alex was being overprotective. But arguing about it would be a waste of time and energy. He checked the contents of the tool bag he carried strapped around his waist.

Amber pointed to Hex's watch. 'You'd better turn off the atomic clock nerd check if you're near those cameras.'

Hex clicked a button on his watch. Then he thought for a moment, took it off and held it out to Alex. 'Can you take this for me?'

Alex gave him a puzzled look. 'Why?'

'I might scratch it if I fall from the tree or something.'

Alex goggled. 'Or you might break your ankle.'

'My ankle is easy to fix; that watch is expensive. Can you just look after it?'

Li wagged her finger at Alex. 'Guard it with your life, now.'

Alex sighed and put the watch on. 'OK. Now can we go?'

Hex nodded. 'Yep. Let's roll.'

They stepped off the road and began to make their way into the undergrowth.

'Good luck,' said Amber, adding, 'Melvin.' She hadn't meant Hex to hear, but he turned round and gave her a withering look. Then he and Alex disappeared into the trees.

The light was starting to fade and the creatures in the undergrowth were gearing up for their dusk chorus. It was like a stopwatch starting the countdown for their mission. Within thirty minutes it would be pitch-dark. Neither Alex nor Hex intended to be out in the jungle after nightfall.

The camera installations had to be as ecologically friendly as possible, so they made use of natural features. They were almost invisible. Alex and Hex knew what they were looking for, however: a tree with a slender metal strut to one side, cleverly hidden by foliage.

They stayed close together. Alex moved in time with Hex, putting his foot down when Hex did, so that if they were picked up on a microphone in the control room it would sound like one person and not two.

Suddenly he tapped Hex on the shoulder. Hex turned and Alex gave the hand signal for 'danger left'. Hex followed his gaze and saw a brown scaly body as thick as his wrist lying in the undergrowth, just where he was about to put his foot. Hex, one foot in the air, adjusted his balance and chose a different route. The snake, sensing the vibrations as they passed, moved away in a rustle of leaves.

They continued carefully and in silence, using hand signals if they needed to communicate, making no more sound than absolutely necessary. Alex loved these moments when Alpha Force worked together so seamlessly; after all their training and practice he and Hex were like two halves of a slick machine. He had thought that he would always be doing this . . .

The tree they were looking for was just ahead. Peering up, they could make out the camera as a box-like outline against a patch of crimson sky. The metal strut had a row of bars sticking out along its length for the technicians to use as a ladder. Alex stood at the bottom of the strut; Hex grasped two of the bars and began to climb.

A moment later he was coming back down again, fast. In answer to Alex's querying expression he pointed upwards. Below the camera Alex spotted the danger coiled through the topmost rungs. At first glance it looked like a cable, but then Alex saw the triangular head moving languidly as the snake tasted the air.

Hex jumped to the ground and began to head further into the jungle. Alex, running to catch up, was taken by surprise. What was he doing? They hadn't discussed a back-up plan. The only reason this camera was a feasible target was that it was reasonably close to the road. Alex couldn't remember where the other cameras were but he was sure they were all much further in. Surely they should simply abort the mission. It was foolhardy to look for another camera – they might not get out before nightfall. But Hex had decided to make a break for it and Alex had no choice but to follow. He muttered some choice words under his breath, fully intending to repeat them to Hex later when they were out of the forest.

Hex moved on ahead. There was no time to waste. If he got to a camera he could splice in the tap without any trouble, and probably make a better job of it than the TV technicians. They would probably let a blip show on the screen and that would give the game away.

That snake was something Hex hadn't bargained for, though, and it had thrown him. He had heard that snakes were sometimes attracted to electrical fields. He hoped that wasn't true. If the next camera was being used as a snake's perch, they might as well give up. By that time the sun would be setting anyway. They wouldn't get another chance.

It took a good five minutes of trekking further into the jungle before Hex and Alex came to another strut. This time Hex peered up to check for snakes before he climbed up the camera support.

To make sure he had a steady hand to work on the camera, he wrapped his legs around the pole and hooked his feet between the rungs. Then he located the cables at the back of the camera and identified which was for power and which for output. They were coated in a sticky substance like thick tar to deter jungle wildlife from chewing them. Hex soon had the stuff all over his fingers. He grimaced at the unpleasant sensation – he really didn't want to get it all over his precision tools. But on the other hand, it was probably a blessing. His fingers were slick with sweat, and the goo made him less likely to drop anything. Just to make sure he didn't slip, Hex wiped some of the stuff onto the insides of his knees and calves as well.

Hex traced the cables to the socket in the back of the camera and prised off the weatherproof cover. He balanced the loose cover in the crook of a branch and scraped some of the anti-chewing goo onto it to make sure it didn't fall. Then he took the bug Sergeant Powell had given him out of his tool pouch.

With his pliers, Hex quickly stripped a length of the output cable. Now he had to splice in the bug without interrupting the signal. This was the tricky part. It didn't help that the light was definitely fading, the sky and the leaf canopy overhead now blurring into one mass of inky darkness.

Hex had to slice into the cable and ensure the cut ends never moved more than a centimetre apart: less than that, and the signal could jump like a spark across the gap; more, and it would register an external fault, which might be enough to rouse Pirroni's suspicions.

Taking a deep breath, Hex cut. Immediately he slotted the signal splitter in between the ends of the severed cable and wrapped his fingers around the whole thing to keep it all together. With his other hand he began to fix the loose ends of the cable into the bug.

Everything was going fine. Hex secured the first end easily and nodded to Alex, looking up from below. Then he became aware of a movement above him, out of his line of vision. A shiver went through him despite the warmth of the jungle.

He looked up and saw the pointed head and seeking tongue, silhouetted against the last wisps of light high in the sky.

Hex stayed very, very still. He knew that if you didn't disturb a snake, it would probably not attack. Very slowly he continued to screw the second cable into the bug. He would get the job finished and then climb down the ladder.

The snake – some kind of python? – began to slide down the back of the camera towards him. Now he could see the spotted markings on its head and back and the pale underbelly. In the dim light he couldn't make out the colour but the light and dark patches were clearly visible. The segments were like fine black lines drawn on its pale skin.

It touched his hand. Hex stayed exactly where he was, trying to think of nothing but holding the cable in the socket. The snake was passing by. He just had to bide his time till it was gone. It was more interested in finding a mouse to eat than in bothering him. It began to travel down his forearm. The scales felt dry and surprisingly warm as it moved over him, and rough like scuffed patent leather.

The coils seemed to be endless, unwinding out of an infinite spool somewhere above the trees. The head was now past Hex's feet and slithering down the trunk of the tree, but still the body kept on coming. His arms and shoulders were burning now with the effort of keeping still. How long could a snake be? Even now that its fangs were past him, he still couldn't risk making any sudden movements because that might endanger Alex on the ground. Grimly he held his position. On and on and on the snake went in an endless leisurely cascade.

The lorry smelled of sweat and hot dogs. A couple of the soldiers were tucking in, knowing they might need the energy at any moment. Nerves seemed to have no effect on their appetite. None of Alpha Force felt particularly hungry, but Amber had got herself a hot dog from the catering truck anyway. As a diabetic she had to stick to regular meal times.

Sergeant Powell had invited them into the makeshift monitoring room. A series of screens were set up on a bench along a wall, wired to the signal from Hex's device.

As they watched, a wobbly picture flashed onto the screens, jumped a bit and settled. Murphy, the SAS soldier who had set the screens up, thumped the desk in triumph. 'Your guy's done it.'

Six monitors showed different views of the camp in dimming light. On one, the door of the control room opened and a figure in flying doctor overalls came out onto the balcony. The cameras in the trees adjusted focus automatically to zoom in on him.

Pirroni put the Colt Commando rifle to his shoulder and surveyed his surroundings, sweeping his weapon around steadily in a wide arc.

Li gasped as it swung directly at the screen. Had he seen something near the cameras?

The figure lowered his rifle, apparently satisfied

there was no danger nearby. He moved forward awkwardly and sat down at the top of the wooden steps with the rifle across his knees.

Paulo and Amber stiffened as they recognized the shuffling gait. Having been so close to him before, they found that seeing him now on screen was rather disturbing. It connected those old stories with the figure they had been chatting to just the day before. They suddenly realized that they were taking part in a fresh chapter of the history of this violent man.

'Sancho Pirroni,' said Sergeant Powell quietly.

'Bet he thinks he's having a nice private think,' Amber mused. 'He's got no idea we can see him.'

'He probably needed to get away from Jonny Cale,' said Li with a grimace.

On the screen, Pirroni seemed to be looking thoughtfully at the cameras. He moved his head slowly to the side as though trying to see round them. For a moment something caught his eye and he remained still. Then he stood up, took his rifle in one hand and went purposefully back into the control room.

'I hope he has not worked out that those cameras can move,' said Paulo.

Alex saw the head of the snake as it slid down the tree trunk. He stayed stock-still. It dropped to the ground near him like a heavy bundle of ship's hawser, slithered past him and disappeared into the undergrowth.

The twilight wouldn't last long at this latitude. Alex was worried about getting back. He mimed a message up to Hex: Are you all right?

Hex, able to move at last, gave the signal for 'OK', then worked like lightning to complete the splice. He snapped the weatherproof cover back on decisively and pattered lightly down the rungs.

Alex signalled: Which way?

Hex indicated. He jogged off into the undergrowth and was almost immediately no more than a shadow in the thickening dusk. Alex started to follow him when a rustle in the undergrowth made him pause. Surely not another snake? He froze so that it could pass.

But the rustle came from above him. Foliage,

disturbed by the movement of the camera. He heard the motor whirring as it rotated and came to rest with its glossy black eye pointing down at him. He heard a mechanical hiss and click as the lens adjusted to look at him. Pirroni had discovered how to use the cameras.

Had he been seen? No point in waiting to find out. Caution didn't matter now. Alex bunched his muscles, ready to sprint in the direction Hex had gone.

A searchlight flared out of the darkness, catching him full in its beam. Alex flung his hands up to shield his eyes. In a split second he thought about dropping to the ground, but decided he would blend in better if he stayed very, very still. Had he been compromised? Cautiously, he opened his eyes. He was on the edge of the clearing in front of the control room. Straight ahead of him was the camp, with a blackened patch where the fire had been. Beyond that was the wooden control room on its stilts.

And standing on the steps with a rifle in his hands was Sancho Pirroni.

11
Captive

Hex hit the undergrowth a moment before the searchlight went on. He flung himself flat and crawled back to look into the clearing. He saw a silhouette against the blinding white light on the side of the control building. Night insects danced and skittered like a thousand dust motes in the beam. Alex stood square in the pool of light, caught like an insect on a pin.

Hex couldn't make out any details in the glare, but he knew the figure had to be Pirroni. Also, from the stance – feet planted solidly, raised shoulders, head slightly cocked to one side – he guessed he was holding a rifle. Obviously Alex had noticed that too, or he would have made a run for it.

Hex saw Alex sink to his hands and knees, feigning exhaustion. 'Thank God I've got back,' he gasped. 'I thought I was lost for good.'

Pirroni was coming down the steps. He'd lowered the rifle now but he still carried it at his hip, trained on Alex. The adrenaline flooding through Hex's system was charging him up to do something. He forced himself to think clearly. Should he rush Pirroni? He had the element of surprise. Pirroni was within a few metres of where Hex was hiding and his back was turned. While the terrorist was busy sizing up his new hostage, his attention was distracted. There wouldn't be a better opportunity to subdue him.

But Pirroni had killed the ranger without compunction. And in London he'd been ambushed by four Special Branch officers. He hadn't been ready for them, and yet all four were dead. Each bullet right between the eyes.

Hex knew he couldn't break cover and pretend he was another of the TV contestants. Pirroni might buy the idea that one had got separated from the group, but two was pushing it. And the toolkit Hex was carrying would be incriminating; it wouldn't take Pirroni long to guess what they had been doing. It would only risk provoking him, and that was a bad idea. He might decide that hurting one of the hostages was the best way to demonstrate that he was still in control.

'Get up the steps,' Pirroni said to Alex.

Alex kept up his act. 'Is this part of the show? Are we on TV?'

Alex allowed Pirroni to prod him towards the control room. Hex knew that Alex's words had been for him as well. Alex was reminding him that their mission was to get a feed from the cameras so that the SAS could see what Pirroni saw.

While the light stayed on, Hex saw he had an advantage. The nearby camera would have adjusted its lens aperture for the floodlights. He could sneak away under cover of darkness. But the light wouldn't stay on for very much longer. He'd have to go right now – abandoning any thought of rescuing Alex. That was the part he didn't like.

Crawling away from the clearing, he found cover behind a tree that was out of sight of any of the cameras. He took out his palmtop and called up a fix on the GPS – the global positioning system that used US navigation satellites to pinpoint a position anywhere in the world. Hex chose a route that would take him well away from the cameras, setting the palmtop to draw a map as he went. Once he had got far enough away he would head back in the direction of the road.

Night had fallen. As Hex crept away from the floodlit clearing, he couldn't make out a thing except the soft glow of the palmtop screen. He moved carefully until his eyes started to adjust and he could see the shapes of the trees. The jungle floor was thick with shadows. Hex remembered diving in a Scottish loch: at the bottom it was murky and dark like this.

His foot caught in a root and he went crashing to the ground. For a moment he lay wincing as pain stabbed up his leg from a twisted ankle. He sat up. His hands were empty.

Panic gripped him. Where was the palmtop? He

couldn't find his way without it. He scanned the dark shapes of the jungle floor, looking for its comforting greenish light. There was nothing. Could the fall have switched it off? He felt around on hands and knees, patting the ground in a circle around where he'd tripped. His hands fell on knobbly branches, dank leaves, small stones . . . Insects wriggled and scuttled away under his touch.

His fingers brushed something hard and smooth. He snatched it up. It was the palmtop. It had fallen face down – that's why he hadn't seen it. The green glow soothed him like a welcoming smile.

Hex stood up. His ankle was throbbing, but he had to press on. Doubts kept whispering from the deepest part of his mind. Shouldn't he have stayed for Alex? Tried to get him away from Pirroni? Or at least hung around to see if he could help? If Alex hadn't insisted on coming in the first place, this would never have happened. Now he might die . . .

No, Hex told himself. That was the reason he and Alex had taken on the mission – so that none of the hostages would die. But now Alex was a hostage too.

Alex walked up the steps ahead of Pirroni. He listened to the uneven footfalls behind him. Although Pirroni had a limp, it didn't seem to slow him down. As Alex reached the door he heard sounds from inside. There was a scuffling on the wooden floor like animals who have been disturbed by a predator, and the sound of panicky whispers. Of course – the hostages had heard one set of footsteps go out, and now an extra set was coming back. They might think that Pirroni was bringing in extra help.

'Put your hands up,' said Pirroni. 'Don't turn round.'

Alex did as he was told. Pirroni saw his knife secured in a sheath on his belt, and the belt pouch containing his survival kit. 'Take off your belt with your left hand and pass it back to me.'

Alex had no choice but to obey. It pained him to hand over the knife; it felt like a part of him. Still holding the rifle, Pirroni slid the knife one-handed out of the sheath and tested its edge by shaving a chunk off the wooden banister. He nodded approvingly, then hooked the sheath to his own belt.

Alex glared over his shoulder. 'That was a present from my father.'

'Then he's a good judge of a knife. Don't turn round again or I'll shoot you.'

Pirroni unzipped the pouch on Alex's belt. His survival kit was in there, sealed in a tobacco tin – also a gift from his father. Pirroni looked at the small oblong tin sealed with waterproof tape, turning it over a couple of times, then slipped it into his pocket.

Alex could think of nothing but the fact that Pirroni had his survival kit and his knife. The former he could replace, but that knife he had looked after for many years. It had seen him through difficult times. It felt like his right hand. He was surprised to find himself almost shaking with anger. He took care not to show it: the first rule in a hostage situation was not to antagonize the captor.

Alex felt the barrel of the rifle nudge him in the back. 'Open the door,' Pirroni ordered.

Alex had to focus on his immediate situation. The contestants had never seen him before. They had only just met each other – were they even all there yet? The presenter had met him only once, briefly, in the control room. Would they give him away? It certainly wouldn't be reasonable to expect six frightened kids in a crisis situation to be able to simply back up a lie. No – he'd have to convince them that he was one of them . . . He turned the handle and pushed the door open. Eight faces looked up at him.

The first thing that hit Alex was the fear. He could see it in the faces, smell it in the air. When he saw these people earlier today on television they had been animated, excited, showing off, goofily spilling water. The vulnerability stamped on those previously carefree faces came as a shock. The eight of them were bunched together in one corner of the room. Some were holding hands, some had their arms around each other. Jonny Cale was cuddling the female journalist.

On one of the screens in front of him, Alex saw the camera's view from outside the building as

Pirroni closed the door. Even if Hex had succeeded in getting a video feed, the SAS soldiers monitoring them could not see inside the control room. Alex and the hostages were on their own.

Pirroni nudged Alex with the stock of his rifle. Looking at Jonny Cale, he said, 'Is this one of the children from the show?'

Jonny Cale shrugged. 'How should I know?' he said. 'I've met so many damn kids in the last few days.'

Alex was thinking fast. He had to act the part. If he had been one of the contestants and had wandered off at dusk only to stumble in on this situation, how would he be reacting now?

'Jonny, what's all this about?' he asked the presenter. 'Is it one of the games?'

Jonny rolled his eyes upwards. 'No, you stupid kid, it's not a game. Now sit down and shut up before you get us all killed.'

At least Jonny hadn't contradicted Alex's story. Alex felt Pirroni's eyes on him. He realized his fate was in the hands of the contestants. He cast his mind back to the shots he had seen earlier of them settling into the camp. He scanned the faces in front of him. He had to remember a name – and something that would convince them he was one of them. There was a girl with pink hair. No, he hadn't seen her before. But, yes, he remembered a girl with very long dark curls that hung like a shawl around her shoulders. He made his voice quieter, less confident. 'Holly,' he said, 'what's happened to your glasses?'

Holly shifted her position to get more comfortable. 'They're still down in the camp. I'm always putting them down and forgetting about them. I don't suppose you saw them when you were out there?'

'Sorry, no, I didn't,' said Alex. 'I was off exploring the forest and didn't realize how late it was getting.'

A girl with the two blonde plaits nodded to Alex as he moved over to the group. 'Here you go, sit here,' she offered, and moved sideways to make a space for him. Alex remembered her name was Milla Davey. 'Move your backside, Woody,' she said. Alex picked his way over and sat down in the gap they had made for him.

'Thanks, Milla.' Alex smiled at her. 'Did we talk earlier? My name's Alex.'

Milla looked at him, frowning as she tried to remember. 'What did you say your father did? Or was it your mother?'

To protect his cover, Alex's parent would have to be famous, of course. But he realized these kids would be familiar with most areas of show business and might ask awkward questions. He needed to choose something they wouldn't be very interested in.

'My dad's a celebrity fitness instructor,' said Alex. Inwardly he grimaced and apologized to his dad. 'Aerobic Vic. You probably won't have seen him,' he added hastily. 'He's on cable.'

'Oh . . . yeah, I remember,' said Milla.

Alex suspected that what she was actually saying was: Now I remember why I didn't find you interesting enough to remember the first time I met you. But all the same he could have kissed her for it. She had corroborated his cover story.

Pirroni had taken up position on one of the two chairs by the door. From there he could see the bank of monitors with their view of the camp perimeter, and he also had a good view of the hostages. He was still looking at Alex, as though weighing up whether he believed him or not.

Eventually he said, 'Yes. I remember you too.'

Alex's mouth went dry. In the car park the day before, right after talking to Amber, Pirroni had got a good look at him. How was he going to get out of this?

'Where?' he said. He couldn't make it look as though he remembered the encounter.

'Out shopping.'

Pirroni was clearly going to say as little as possible and watch how Alex reacted. Alex had to make sure he didn't betray any extra knowledge. 'I'm sorry, I don't remember. When was it?'

Pirroni was looking at him with the same expression Alex remembered from the car park. The same intense, probing telepathic stare. 'Yesterday,' he said. 'Before these other kids arrived, come to think of it.'

'I came long haul from the UK. I wanted a couple of days to get over the jet lag,' said Alex. 'I did a bit of exploring yesterday.'

Pirroni seemed satisfied with that – as far as Alex could tell.

In the monitoring room, Li, Amber and Paulo watched in horrified silence as Pirroni escorted Alex up the steps and into the control room.

Murphy stared at the screen in surprise. 'Where did he come from? Might have been better staying lost. Sergeant, should we get the negotiator to phone?'

'No,' said Sergeant Powell. 'It might look as though we've orchestrated it and the kid will suffer.'

Amber glanced at Sergeant Powell. His face was expressionless. She understood what that meant. He had made it clear it was a deniable mission. No-one should know he had sent Alex and Hex in. But it wasn't long before Pirroni rang them. The ring tone came through as a crackle on the speaker attached to the computer.

The negotiator was alone in the trailer next door. He was deliberately isolated to give the terrorist the impression that he was working on his own and that their conversation was private: background noise could give away vital plans, or the terrorist could get spooked if he thought a roomful of people were monitoring his every word. However, the negotiator was in closed-message contact with the other trailer, in case they needed to send him information.

He answered the call smoothly, his voice welcoming. It was part of the technique to befriend the hostage-taker. 'Is that you, Peter?' he asked. Even though he knew Pirroni's real identity, he used the name the terrorist had been living under when in hiding. It helped create an atmosphere of trust.

'It is.'

'How is everyone?'

'They are fine,' replied Pirroni. He eased himself into a sitting position on the top step.

'What can I do for you?'

In the hostage stronghold, Alex was listening. His fingers strayed to Hex's watch on his wrist and he remembered the interference caused by the time-checking device. Experimentally, he turned it on, then peered up at the monitors. Sure enough, it caused a blip on the screen. He wondered if he could control it. He turned it off again. The picture became clear and smooth. He clicked the button on again, this time holding it down. The blip lasted for longer. That was good, thought Alex.

Amber was looking at the screen, matching the plan to the wide-angle view, when the picture seemed to hiccup. It was like an eye blinking at her. Then it blinked again.

Paulo was sitting nearest to her. She touched him on the arm and pointed. 'Look.'

They looked at the screen, willing it to happen again. It did. This time it was longer.

'Alex,' said Paulo quietly. He touched Li's arm and indicated the screen. He mouthed Alex's name at her. Relief flooded through her face like a light.

Pirroni's voice crackled through the speaker. 'I have a new hostage.'

Paulo still had his hand on Li's arm. The fingers tightened.

'Tell me about him,' said Pirroni.

'I don't personally know any of the people you have with you at the moment,' said the negotiator.

'However, if you give me your questions, I can find you the answers and get back to you.'

Pirroni asked his question: 'Just tell me this. What does this new kid's father do?'

In the monitoring room Amber, Li and Paulo saw the screens start to blink rapidly.

Paulo said quietly. 'Alex is trying to get a message to us.'

'Could be Morse code,' said Amber in a low voice. 'Damn! It's years since I did any for sailing. Now we just use satellite phones.'

Sergeant Powell had been listening to Amber, Li and Paulo. He barked an order: 'Murphy, can you take down that message?'

Murphy seized a pen and started to scribble down dots and dashes, translating them into letters as he went.

Li noticed that Murphy was looking puzzled. What he was writing seemed to be gobbledegook. 'Can the negotiator keep Pirroni talking?' she asked Powell. 'The hostages are trying to get a message through.'

Sergeant Powell hit a key on the keyboard in front of him. It sent a code to the other room.

The negotiator asked his next question smoothly, as though it was completely natural to keep talking. 'While you're here, Peter, is there anything you need? Water? Food?'

'We don't need anything. Except what I asked you for.'

'Do you have any family you would like us to get a message to?'

'You know my needs,' said Pirroni. They could see on the screen that he looked irritated, and it came through in his voice. 'I want a car with a police escort and safe passage to a neutral territory. Have you got that for me?'

The negotiator's voice was patient. 'Some of the things you are asking for will take time. They're not directly within my power. I have to ask government officials. However, if you're prepared to be patient, I'm sure things will work out. I need you to bear with me so that this goes as smoothly as possible for everyone. Can you do that?'

Alex, sitting on the floor of the control room, had heard the question. He wished his thumbs could signal faster. The button was fiddly and he was in danger of turning a dot into a dash. He prayed Pirroni would keep talking so that he could transmit a meaningful message. Once he came back in he was bound to notice what Alex was doing. He clicked away on the button and prayed someone was receiving him.

Then he heard something he didn't want to hear: Pirroni said, 'Goodbye.'

12
Alone in the Dark

In the monitoring room the screens became steady again.

'They heard him come off the phone and had to stop,' said Murphy. He was looking down at the pad on which he'd scribbled Alex's message. 'But this doesn't make sense.'

The door to the lorry opened and the negotiator walked in. 'I'm sorry,' he said. 'I couldn't keep him.' He was grey-haired, in his fifties, and his face looked tired and haggard.

Murphy was shaking his head.

Sergeant Powell stood up. 'Leave that,' he told Murphy. 'Not many kids know Morse these days. I doubt they even knew we were picking anything up, much less that they intended it to make sense.'

'We can easily find out what his dad does, surely?' said Murphy.

Sergeant Powell thumped the desk. 'What we need is a way in past those cameras. That's what's going to save those kids, not answering twenty questions. Then if he starts shooting or makes a run for it, we can take him down. We'll send two snipers in as close as we can. We keep pushing the government to let us use force and stage an assault. The monitors are a big breakthrough. We can see if the kids are inside and safe.'

He turned to the negotiator. 'When we get the nod, you can call him on the phone. Tell him you're about to meet his demands, so he'll want to listen. We'll put some crackle on it to sound like the reception's bad. When he walks to the bottom of the steps and away from the kids to get better reception, we nail him. Unless anyone has any other ideas . . .'

Murphy nodded. 'He's going to have to come out soon. He's got no supplies.'

Amber looked at Paulo and Li. They weren't part of this discussion any more. She nodded towards the door, then got up. The others followed her out.

Outside it was dark. 'Look at this, guys,' said Amber. She turned her head towards the sky, where the tree canopy was silhouetted against the darkening sky. 'Is Hex still out in this?'

Paulo put a soothing hand on her arm. 'He's got his palmtop. He can use the GPS.'

They had sat down on the steps of the nearby field ambulance, but now Amber stood up again and started to pace. 'I can't keep still at a time like this. And fancy Alex sending a message that was rubbish.'

'I don't think he'd have sent a message that was rubbish,' said Paulo.

'Neither do I,' said Li firmly. 'He sent it after Pirroni asked the question about his father.'

'He may simply have been telling us not to say what his father really does – not to say he's in the SAS,' said Paulo.

'No, I think he was trying to say something,' said Li. 'If Pirroni doesn't get a satisfactory answer to his question, he will be suspicious of Alex. If the SAS get the all-clear to go in, that may not matter.'

'But if they don't,' said Amber, 'what does Alex do?'

The chorus of animals was dying down. The jungle was going to sleep. Hex was making progress but it was painfully slow. He was confident that he was clear of the cameras, but now he had to get back to the road. He trod carefully, stopping for every rustle and movement. The memory of the snake on the camera kept haunting him; the feel of its strong, muscular body as it slid over him. It could have stopped at any moment and squeezed the life out of him.

How dark was it? Hex realized he was having to use the screen from his palmtop as a torch. He stopped and looked around. It was really dark now. Hex tried to tell himself it wasn't, but it was. When he looked away from the palmtop it was like he had black material pressed up against his face. Panic began to well up inside him. He felt as if he was in a confined space, suffocating. He glanced down at his palmtop again. The panic receded a little, became more controllable.

He stepped onwards, carefully. At least with the GPS he could see he was making progress.

Something touched his face. And then he felt something that he had been dreading. Something heavy dropped onto his neck and around his shoulders. It was large, brawny and solid. He let out a yell and his hands tore at it, but still more of it tumbled down onto him. He struggled and wriggled, fired by pure panic. He realized that it was one of those constrictors – if he didn't get out quickly that would be the end of him. It was coiled loosely around his body, his legs, bumping against them as he tried to jerk his way out. It slithered off his shoulders, brushed down against his arms and fell heavily around his feet. He leaped sideways and managed to get free.

Incredibly, he hadn't lost his palmtop. It was stuck to his calves, on the sticky stuff he had picked up from the cables. He prised it off his trousers and decided to attach it to his left forearm. The light from the screen flashed off another shape hanging in the darkness. It was very close to Hex's ear. He turned slowly. He brought his left arm up in an automatic gesture of defence and saw . . . a rope.

It was hanging in the trees. Next to it was another. Feeling a bit braver, he crouched down and shone the palmtop light on the ground. Another rope.

It wasn't a snake that had attacked him earlier, it was a rope. He had blundered into one of the games.

Relief flooded through him. He walked on again, feeling fragile and battered, as though his nerves had gone through a shredder several times. The hardest thing was that he was alone.

A thought occurred to him. He began to type. Hex had many friends throughout the world on the Net, and now he sent out a desperate plea into the ether. 'Is anyone there?'

Two replies came instantly: 'Hi, Hex, it's sunny, I'm sitting by the pool working on my tan. Whaddya doing?' Hex clicked to the next message. 'Hi, Hex, save me! I'm in a meeting. It's boring and it's going to be boring for another two hours. Tell me something amazing before my brain strangles me out of revenge.' Hex mailed back: 'I'm doing something very exciting and hating it. Tell me something boring.'

Hex took a few deep breaths. OK, he was not alone any more. He flipped to the GPS screen and resumed his journey. Still taking every step with the utmost care, he sent short messages to friends around the globe. Using the little keyboard while giving a task his full concentration was second nature to Hex. He kept the GPS program on view to make sure he was still on course. Then he would flip to his e-mail to see if he had another reply. Little did those correspondents know that their words were a vital lifeline. It could only be another few minutes, Hex told himself. Not far now.

The lights were on in the control room. Outside was pitch dark, which made the wooden room seem tiny and claustrophobic.

Pirroni went out onto the veranda again.

Milla Davey voiced what was on all their minds.

'Look how dark it is,' she said quietly. 'How long are we going to be here?'

It was Sarah Compton, the journalist, who replied. 'What if we're here all night?' She kept scratching at the bite she had wanted the doctor to look at. At least it didn't seem to be getting worse.

Milla was huddling against Holly, her arm around the smaller girl. She squeezed her tighter, seeking comfort. 'Surely we won't be here that long,' she said.

Alex was working fast. He had seen Pirroni take a packet of cigarettes from the console and estimated the terrorist would be outside for a couple of minutes at least. He pressed the switch on Hex's watch and tried sending his message again. Out of the corner of his eye he could see the screens flicker. He knew he ran the risk of Pirroni noticing, but he had to take the chance.

'What are you doing?' asked Zoe Patterson. The pink streak in her hair looked even brighter under the strip lights. Her face looked pale with strain.

Alex shrugged. 'Sorry. It's a thing I do when I'm nervous.' He carried on clicking away, struggling to remember the Morse. It was tricky to do that and talk at the same time.

'That's a cool watch,' said Mark Roland. He was sitting next to Zoe and peering around her to get a closer look. 'Can I see it?'

Alex was right in the middle of his message. He didn't want to stop sending while he had the chance, and he also didn't want to let anyone know what he was up to in case they accidentally betrayed him to Pirroni. He would have to cover up what he was doing. 'Hang on a moment,' he said. 'I've reset something and I have to keep clicking until it's back to normal.' He tutted and muttered to himself as he finished the message. Then he clicked the time-check function off and took the watch off his wrist to let Mark look at it.

'Cool,' said Mark. 'Why are you wearing another?' he said.

Alex realized his own watch was peeking out of his shirt cuff. He pulled back his arm self-consciously. 'That one belongs to my girlfriend,' he said. It was the first thing that came into his head. 'She wanted me to wear it, but it's not as accurate as the other one.' He knew it sounded lame and grimaced to himself.

'Won't she see you're wearing both watches? Like, doh, you're on TV!' said Zoe.

'She knows,' was all Alex could think of to say.

'I suppose the fact that you're wearing it is like a message,' said Milla Davey. 'That you love her, I mean,' she added, seeing the look on Alex's face. 'That's what counts.' She was fiddling with her plaits, undoing the ends and then braiding them again.

Zoe was huddled up to Mark. She said in a quiet voice, 'We should be doing something. Not just sitting here. I mean, I feel so helpless. How long do we just sit and wait?'

Alex glanced at the door. The figure outside remained still. A curl of smoke drifted in. He kept his voice low when he replied. 'People know we're here. It's being sorted out. We just need to sit tight.'

Zoe snorted. 'How do you know that?'

Alex had to think quickly again. 'Because they keep phoning him. They're asking him what he wants.'

'The TV company sure as hell knows we're here,' drawled Jonny Cale. 'They've had to take the programme off the air. It was going to go out every night. It'll have made a hell of a hole in the schedule.' Jonny spoke with a worldly-wise swagger, but underneath it all Alex could see he was as scared as the rest of them.

'What if they don't give him what he wants?' whispered Zoe fiercely. 'What happens to us? Does anyone care? We're just a bunch of pawns. How long do we just sit here?'

Some of the others looked daggers at Zoe and hissed at her to be quiet. There was real fear in their eyes. Peter Bailey and Woody Brasher had been silent throughout the whole episode. They seemed to have shut down, almost as if they were hoping the situation would just go away. According to Alex's dad, that was how some people reacted in sieges. Others became frustrated at their powerlessness, which was dangerous for two reasons – it might provoke their captor into premature action, and it undermined the morale of the rest of the hostages. Of the two approaches, Peter's and

Woody's was the more sensible. Zoe was right – they *were* pawns; the best thing they could all do was stay quiet and let the SAS solve the problems.

'Listen, guys,' said Alex. 'We're doing the right thing. We have to stay calm. Nobody must even think about escaping or heroics. If we do that, he'll kill someone.'

Mark looked incredulous. 'We just sit here, is that it?' he whispered.

Alex nodded. 'Think of it this way. We think it's just the nine of us here against him. But outside there are lots of people trying to get us out. We don't have to try and get out – it's *their* job to do that.' From the angle of the smoke curling in through the door he could see that Pirroni was listening. So far what he'd said should reassure the terrorist as well as the hostages. Alex didn't mention the SAS; that might make Pirroni panic.

'Well, why haven't they got us out yet?' retorted Jonny.

'It takes time. They can't always get what he wants immediately. Trust me. If we sit quietly and wait, we *will* get out.'

'How do you know so much about it?' said Milla.

'My dad trains bodyguards,' replied Alex. At least that was not a lie.

Holly asked him, 'How long do you think this will go on for?'

Alex thought carefully. Now it was dark, he doubted they would be released before morning, if then. Should he tell them they were definitely there for the night? Peter and Woody would cope, but some of the others might panic. On the other hand, if the night dragged on and nothing happened, their fear might boil up into even more frustration. No, he would gain credibility if he told them. If the siege carried on for days, they had to keep believing he was right when he said they had to sit quietly.

'Listen, guys. I've no idea how long we will be here. But I can guarantee we will be here for the night. Nothing can move in the jungle at night, so they can't get him a boat or a car or whatever he wants yet.'

Eight faces looked back at him. Peter and Woody looked stoical. The others looked at him with varying degrees of horror.

'It's not a sign that it's all going wrong,' Alex continued, 'or that they've abandoned us. You'll hear them phoning him from time to time, and that's a sign that they're still looking after us. But nothing can happen until morning. The best thing to do now is get some sleep.'

13

Code-breakers

'Another message has come through. More gobbledegook.' Sergeant Powell held out a crumpled piece of paper to Li, Paulo and Amber, who were still sitting on the steps of the ambulance. Li reached up and took it. She unfolded it and smoothed the creases out over her leg with the palm of her hand.

Amber peered at the message. She saw a mass of capital letters. 'Is this Alex or a monkey with a typewriter?'

The sergeant turned to go. 'See what you can

make of it. By the way, officially I didn't give this to you.'

Paulo nodded. 'Absolutely.'

'I'm afraid we're short staffed so there's no-one to take you back at the moment. You can work in my trailer, and if you need to get some sleep there are some tents just beyond the ambulance. Help yourselves to a crash pallet any time you want.' He walked over to the surveillance trailer.

They hurried across to Powell's trailer. Li pulled the door open and turned on the lights. The others followed her in.

'Phew, smells a bit in here,' said Amber, wafting her hand in front of her face. The lorry was as rank as the surveillance lorry and the waste-paper basket was full of greasy wrappers. 'These guys sure like their hot dogs.'

Paulo pulled out a chair, then suddenly heard excited voices outside. He paused, his hand still on the back of the chair.

'What's that?' said Li.

Amber opened the door. A policeman was talking to one of the SAS soldiers. There was another figure with him, but his face was obscured. Amber managed to catch what the policeman was saying: 'This kid just came out of the jungle. He must be one of the contestants and he's been hiding all this time.'

Amber stepped out of the trailer to get a better view. The 'kid' was Hex.

Hex saw her too. He gave her a brief glance and then looked away.

Amber understood. It was easier if the other soldiers and police thought he was an escaped contestant; otherwise they might ask difficult questions about what he was doing in the jungle.

Discreetly, she used one of their hand signals. 'You OK?'

Hex saw and signalled back: 'OK.'

Sergeant Powell stepped out of the surveillance trailer. 'Is that one of the kids?' he said. 'I'll debrief this one.'

'We've got to get our skates on,' said Amber. She closed the lorry door and pulled out a chair.

'What's happened?' said Li. She was writing out the transcriptions of Alex's messages on a clean sheet of paper so that they could read them more clearly.

'Hex is back and being debriefed,' said Amber. She cracked her knuckles together, limbering up for work. 'Think how annoyed he'll be if we crack these codes without him.'

'OK,' grinned Li. 'I'll read them out, see if they make sense that way. Y-D-C-L-B-I-K-N-V-R-C-T-R – that's the first; and S-Y-D-C-L-B-F-T-N-S-T-R-C-T-R. Not exactly clear, is it?'

Paulo picked up Li's pencil and started writing one of them out backwards, then scribbled it out. 'No, he wouldn't be deliberately trying to make them difficult.'

'I knew Alex's spelling was bad,' said Li gloomily, 'but . . .'

'The question is,' said Amber, 'is it his spelling that's bad, or his Morse?'

'If it is both, we are really in trouble,' said Paulo.

Li picked up the pencil again. 'Why don't I try writing the letters in a circle, like when you solve an anagram—'

Paulo shook his head. 'No, Li, you're barking up

the wrong tree. The solution has to be simple. He wants to be understood, not to set us challenges.'

Amber sat back and let out a sigh. 'Maybe it's Nurthumbrian,' she said, attempting an imitation of Alex's accent. She was fed up that they were getting nowhere.

'Nor'oom'rian,' corrected Li.

Paulo had to laugh. Li's attempt to mimic Alex was uncannily accurate.

'Listen, guys, this is serious,' said Amber.

'Both these messages look similar,' said Paulo. 'I think they are the same message, repeated.'

'It might still be rubbish, though,' said Amber. 'A warning to tell us not to let Pirroni know his father's a soldier. Like clearing your throat to stop someone saying something tactless.'

'That's possible, but I think it's more than mere throat-clearing,' said Paulo. He frowned as he looked at the message again. Then his expression changed. 'Wait a minute . . . Suppose it was a text message. Look at the second one.'

Li's face became more animated. 'Aha,' she said, and began to scribble under the letters. 'It's about his father, right? D must be "Dad". Could it be "Say Dad"?'

'That's good,' said Paulo. 'He's probably left the vowels out, so . . . that last bit could be "instructor"—'

'Brilliant,' said Li, and wrote it down.

Paulo frowned. 'But what is a "clb ft instructor"?'

'Club foot?' said Amber absently, and immediately shook her head. Then she banged the table triumphantly. 'Got it! The last bit could be "fit instructor". And I bet C-L-B is "celeb" because he'd have to say something to fit in with all the other contestants. It's "celebrity fitness instructor"!'

Li was on her feet and snatching up the piece of paper. 'I'll get this to Sergeant Powell straight away. It could get Alex out of trouble.' She opened the door and jumped out.

'But what about this?' Paulo pointed to the other version.

Amber was on a roll. 'That was his first attempt, wasn't it? And it looks similar. When I was doing Morse I kept getting the timing wrong. You have to leave a space of one unit – a second or whatever of silence – to indicate a new letter, otherwise they run together and you get different letters. One thing I remember is that if you don't put a space between S and T, you get V, and if you put F and T together you can get I and K. If you compare the first message and the second . . .'

Paulo was already with her: '. . . and if you leave the S off the beginning, they're the same!'

Amber folded her arms and let her head fall forwards onto them. 'That was like pulling teeth,' she groaned. 'Next time, we'll let Hex do it, OK?'

'First of all let's check you haven't been bitten by anything,' said Sergeant Powell. 'Come with me.' He led Hex towards the ambulance.

For Hex, it was such a relief to be walking on solid surfaces like tarmac, and to be surrounded by light. He no longer had to be careful of whispering dark leaves and scuttling creatures.

He had emerged from the jungle onto the road, straight into the police cordon. He had stood there, dazzled by the searchlights, while they decided he must be an escaped contestant. A policeman had escorted him, with great excitement, to the SAS camp. For the moment Hex had no objections to being treated like a returning hero, but then he thought of Alex, still in the forest. The knowledge that he had left him there returned like a bitter taste.

Sergeant Powell opened the back door of the green ambulance and showed Hex in. Hex climbed up and sat gratefully on one of the stretchers. When he touched the soft surface his brain seemed to stop and beg for sleep. He felt exhausted.

Sergeant Powell closed the door. He looked at Hex and said, 'Well done.'

'Is it working?'

The sergeant nodded. 'It's working.'

Hex peeled his palmtop off his shirt sleeve. Its screen bore the trace of the route he had taken back to civilization. 'You know you couldn't get snipers in because the cameras would see you? You can now.' With his finger he traced his route – a wiggly line like the outline of a jigsaw puzzle, and then a fairly straight line. 'This straight bit is clear of the night-vision cameras. You can get men to here without being seen.'

'And then what?'

'You turn on the spotlights.' Despite his exhaustion, Hex managed a grin. 'I got away because the spotlights in the main camp came on. They wiped out the cameras' night vision. If you can do that, you can get to within forty metres of the control room.'

Sergeant Powell nodded. 'That's close enough for the snipers. How do we turn on the lights?'

'They're motion triggered.'

Sergeant Powell clenched his fist as his excitement mounted. 'So we can drop something in by parachute . . .'

Hex picked up on his wavelength. 'It's got to be quite big. They were set so they wouldn't come on just for a small animal.'

Sergeant Powell was already moving. He stepped out of the ambulance, talking to Hex over his shoulder. 'He's asked for water. I'll get the negotiator to tell him we're dropping it in by parachute. I'll scramble a floatplane from HQ.' He paused before he walked away and added, 'Stay there. You need to be examined. You'd better drink some water too.'

* * *

There was a heavy thump outside. Alex woke with a start. On either side of him Holly and Zoe jumped as though electrocuted. Zoe grabbed him, he grabbed Holly. They all stared at each other in shock.

Pirroni was immediately out on the veranda. There was a shot. The camp lights came on.

Alex was surrounded by screaming, terrified faces. It was like a painting of hell. Eyes were wide and pleading for mercy. Hands were grabbing flesh as though holding onto another person would keep them alive.

Then the screaming subsided and became a frightened silence. Outside was silent too.

Alex took a deep breath and calmed himself. 'Shhh,' he said. He cautiously raised himself to his knees and peered out of the window.

'What is it?' said Sarah.

Alex looked back at her. 'It's a big crate on a parachute.'

He heard Pirroni come back towards the door and sat down rapidly. The terrorist came in. The whole room held its breath. Each of the hostages flinched as he looked at them. After a moment he pointed at Woody Brasher. 'You. Come here.'

In the monitoring room Murphy and Sergeant Powell watched as Pirroni limped awkwardly down the steps. Woody Brasher walked in front of him. His face looked ashen against his dark hair.

The crate had landed in the middle of the camp. The parachute was floating down in clouds of white nylon. Pirroni put his gun to Woody's back and nudged him towards the crate. The captive obeyed, moving in a stilted way, as though operated by remote control.

The SAS men watched the screen as Pirroni and Woody retrieved the water supplies, then went back up the stairs into the control room.

Ten seconds after the lights came on, a message came through on the secure audio frequency: 'Snipers in position.'

Paulo put his head round the door of the ambulance. 'Hex, there you are!'

'What are you doing on your own in here?' said Amber.

Hex was rubbing his eyes. He'd dozed off. Was Sergeant Powell back? His three friends were peering at him from the doorway. Not four? Why no Alex? Then he remembered.

He shifted into a sitting position. His neck was stiff. 'I'm waiting for a medical. They're worried I might have got bitten by something while I was crawling around in the dark.'

'Quite right too,' said Paulo, and climbed in. 'Often you don't realize you've been bitten by a snake until later when you swell up. Do you feel sick, or do you itch anywhere?' He tilted Hex's head back and looked into his pupils.

Hex, still groggy, allowed himself to be moved around like a doll. 'No, but I could do with some sleep.'

Paulo's voice was firm. 'Examination first. Sleep later. Take off your shirt.'

Hex was about to shake him off. This was too much. Then he thought about the numerous snakes he'd encountered. Perhaps it was a good idea after all. He began to undo his shirt buttons.

'Paulo, do you know how to check for snake

bites?' Li asked from the doorway. Her voice was sceptical.

Paulo picked up Hex's arm and began inspecting. 'I used to check the horses and cattle on the ranch.'

'They're not quite like people,' said Li.

Paulo grinned. 'People are a lot easier because they are less hairy.'

'Some are,' said Amber dubiously. 'Look at that chest.'

Hex knew he should insult her in return, but he didn't have the energy. He was weary to his very soul. All he could think about was how he had left Alex to be taken hostage. He looked around at all the grinning faces. They all seemed pleased to see him, but what did they really think of him for coming back alone?

An unmistakable noise drifted in on the night breeze. 'Hey,' said Amber, 'was that a plane?' She turned and looked up.

'It must be the SAS returning from their supply drop,' said Hex. 'It was cover to get some snipers in.'

Li was looking in the direction of the plane. 'I think I can see its lights. Where's it landing?'

Paulo looked at Hex. He sensed he needed to talk one to one, but how was he going to get rid of the others? He put his hand on the ambulance doors. 'The next part of the examination, girls, is not for your eyes. Hex, get your trousers off.' He closed the doors gently but firmly.

'Meanie,' said Amber to the closed doors.

'Boys' talk,' sighed Li.

The crash tents formed ghostly peaks beyond the ambulance. Amber suddenly realized how tired she was. 'There's nothing more we can do at the moment,' she yawned. 'I'm going to turn in while we've got the chance. That's if I can find a tent that doesn't contain a soldier snoring his boots off.'

'OK. I'm not tired yet but I'll be along in a bit,' said Li.

In the ambulance, Paulo fixed his eyes on Hex. 'So,' he said, 'you're a complete coward because you ran off and left Alex.'

Hex looked stunned. 'What?'

'That's what you're saying to yourself. Just listen

to how it sounds when I say it. That's not the whole story, is it? There's more to it than that.'

Hex nodded. 'I suppose you're right, but—'

'But nothing.' Paulo was adamant. 'It wouldn't have done any good for you to get caught too. You know that. Then we would have been two men down. As it was, you got out with vital information. And we're going to save Alex too, OK?'

'You're right,' said Hex. 'I'm tired; I wasn't thinking straight.'

'We're all tired,' said Paulo. He smiled, relieved that his shock therapy had snapped Hex out of it. 'Let's get some sleep so we can tackle this fresh in the morning.'

Li didn't feel tired. She went up the road and a little way into the darkness beyond the arc lights, jogging as the cold of the jungle night hit her. On one side the shadowy trees disappeared and in their place was the lake, a silvery slick of water stretching into the black distance. Two rows of lights were strung along the shore to make an aquatic landing strip. The plane bobbed gently between the lights, tethered near the road. Two soldiers were loading it with supplies.

Why was that, she wondered? Could Pirroni have asked for it?

Li sat down and watched them. She saw a crate of water bottles go in, then the soldier stepped out of the cabin carrying a box of equipment. So they were removing things too. That definitely suggested someone might be taking it away. The two soldiers climbed up the bank and walked back towards the camp.

Li went closer, stepping carefully down the bank and peered into the cabin. It was empty. Cautiously she climbed in. A little illumination came from the landing lights along the shore. The plane was about the size of the ambulance inside, with shadowy bunks along each side, their lids propped open. The pallet of water bottles stood on the floor. There was more than enough for one person. The plane was quite big, too. That could only mean he was going to take the hostages with him.

She went closer to one of the bunks and inspected it. There was a blanket in the bottom, and enough room for someone small to hide. An idea came to her suddenly. If she could stow away, maybe she could help Alex and the hostages.

She climbed carefully out of the plane and jogged back to find the others. First stop was the ambulance. She put her ear to the cold metal of the door. All was quiet; Hex and Paulo were no longer talking. Cautiously, she pushed it open.

Paulo was sitting up, but asleep, his head lolling to one side. It looked as though he would have a painful stiff neck in the morning. Hex's feet were visible on the other side of him. Li peered in further. The hacker was curled in a foetal position, his face buried in his arms. They both were deeply asleep.

She closed the door quietly. Maybe Amber was still awake. She went to the nearest tent, pulled aside the canvas flap and put her head in.

The first thing she noticed was a fuggy smell of sweaty bodies and hot-dog halitosis. There were five camp beds, two of them containing bodies. One looked small enough to be Amber, although its head was buried in the pillow. As Li looked it turned over, revealing Amber's ebony features. She mumbled quietly and put her arm over her forehead. She was obviously deeply asleep too.

Li pulled her head out again and went to sit on the ambulance steps. Her brain was buzzing. Should she wake the others to discuss it? They were all obviously very tired. The plane only had room for one stowaway and that person had to be as small as possible. If she did discuss it they would agree that it had to be her. She could just go ahead anyway. But should she, without consulting them? They were a team and it wasn't very professional. On the other hand, they might lose the chance if she didn't act now . . .

That decided it. She took a notepad and pen out of her shirt pocket and scribbled a message: 'I've gone with the plane to help the hostages – Li'.

She crept into the tent and crossed to Amber's sleeping form. She knelt by the head of the bed. Amber didn't stir, but breathed deeply and steadily. This confirmed to Li that she was doing the right thing. If Paulo and Hex were like that too it would take a good ten or twenty minutes to get them all awake and able to make a decision. She tucked the message under Amber's pillow and made her way out.

The cool night air refreshed her after the stale air of the tent. She set off for the plane.

14
Escape

The tent smelled stale. Light filtered through the green canvas, making everything look ghostly. The bed was a simple piece of canvas, like a hammock in an oblong frame, but Amber felt brighter and more rested now. She checked the time: it was nearly six o'clock. Four other beds were set up in a row along the tent and all of them were empty. Li must be up already.

Amber felt under the bed for her belt pouch and injected her morning dose of insulin. The pillow moved and dislodged Li's note. It fluttered to the floor unseen.

Amber pulled her boots on. Next task was to find breakfast. If the catering lorry wasn't up and running, she'd go and make something herself.

Outside there was a new arrival. A tanker painted in army camouflage was parked in the middle of the road, its engine running. A thick black pipe led out of its side and snaked onto the road; the paraffin smell of aviation fuel wafted towards her. A soldier was standing beside a panel on the chassis, monitoring the fuel delivery. 'G'day,' he said to Amber.

'Hi there,' she smiled back.

Curious, she followed the pipe. It ran off the road through the trees, down the bank by the lake, dipped into the water for a metre or so and emerged to hook into the fuel inlet of a blue and white seaplane. 'So that's where it landed,' said Amber. The craft looked like a delicate bird, its slender body supported by four struts and resting on two white floats.

Her stomach rumbled. She turned back. 'Breakfast,' she said to herself firmly.

Sergeant Powell hurried past her, then hesitated and turned round. He spoke rapidly. 'We got back to the target with your decode of your mate's message, so he should be in the clear. Well done! However, last night Pirroni changed his demands. He wants a plane immediately. So Alex might soon be out anyway.' Then he called to the soldier at the refuelling lorry. 'I want the plane marked so we can spot it from the ground.'

'Very good, sir.'

Amber spotted Hex and Paulo just emerging from their tents and jogged over to tell them the news. 'Oh,' said Hex. 'Is Li not with you?'

'Haven't you seen her?' asked Amber. 'She must be in the other tent.' In the green gloom she saw four canvas beds. One had an occupant but it was much too big to be Li.

'I looked in the other one and she's not there either,' said Paulo. 'Where can she be?'

'Maybe she's helping with breakfast,' said Amber, glaring at him. 'Hint.'

Pirroni was on the phone. 'Is my plane ready?'

The hostages were all awake, listening. Alex strained, but he couldn't hear the negotiator's reply.

'I want that plane at six-thirty,' said Pirroni. 'If it is not ready then, I will shoot a hostage. For every twenty minutes you delay after that, I will shoot another.'

Alex felt fingers curl painfully into his arms like claws. Milla and Holly clung onto him for dear life. He leaned forward and spoke softly but emphatically. 'Stay calm. No heroics. It won't be long now. Remember your job is to stay alive until you can be rescued.'

Eight frightened faces nodded back at him.

Sergeant Powell was in direct contact with six snipers via an earpiece. Two were next to the main camp. Four more had come in with the fuel lorry that morning and were in key points around the lake, where Pirroni was to get into the plane. If they could get a clear shot at the target, they would take him out. But not if it meant endangering the hostages. Their safety was paramount and to date the operation had been successful. No hostage had yet lost their life. The SAS wanted to keep it that way!

The negotiator was in the other lorry, ready. He had made the arrangements with Pirroni, but even at this late stage the terrorist might change his demands.

Hex, Amber and Paulo were in the field ambulance, sitting in a row along the stretcher. Hex had his arms round a computer monitor, feeling for a socket with his fingers. He found it and inserted a plug. Then he flicked a key on his palmtop with a flourish and the monitor sprang into life. 'Now,' he grinned, 'we can see what's on the cameras. I'm tuned into the signal splitter.'

'Hey, cool,' said Amber.

'I still wonder where Li's got to.' Paulo sounded worried.

'She must be helping Sergeant Powell; that's the only place we haven't looked,' said Amber.

'Shh, look.' Hex nodded towards the monitor. 'They're coming out.'

The door of the control room opened.

'Jeez, look at them,' said Amber.

A hostage stepped out onto the wooden steps, wearing a grey ski mask that covered the whole head like a balaclava, leaving only the eyes showing in a sinister narrow slit.

'Who's that?' asked Hex.

'Looks like one of the big guys,' said Paulo. 'Mark, or what's his name? – Woody.'

'Pirroni's put that on everyone,' said Amber. 'Look.' Another hostage followed the first, and another, all wearing the same grey masks.

'He's made them all look the same,' said Hex. 'The snipers will just about be able to tell who's male and who's female, but not much else. Is he planning a diversion?'

Amber stabbed at the screen with her finger. 'I think that one's Alex.' She pointed at a tall, rangy figure coming down the steps.

'And guess who that is behind him,' Paulo mused. The next figure to leave wore the flying doctor overalls as well as a ski mask. He limped as he came down the steps. Paulo squinted and leaned forwards. 'Is that . . . ? He's got a gun.' Poking out of the sleeve of the overalls was the black tip of a gun muzzle.

Hex fiddled with a switch. There was a crackle from the computer's speaker and words started to come through. 'Target has been sighted. He is armed. Stand by.'

'That's the reports from the snipers,' explained Hex. He couldn't help but grin proudly.

'Hey, sound as well as vision,' said Amber. 'You must have been up early.' She looked back at the screen. 'But tell me this. What's the point of Pirroni putting those masks on them since he's wearing those overalls and the snipers will know him by his limp anyway?'

Alex walked slowly, in time with the others. The ski mask was itchy; underneath, his mouth was sealed with a silver length of duct tape. He followed behind Zoe, Holly, Milla, Mark, Peter and Woody. But the limping figure immediately breathing down his neck was not Pirroni. It was Jonny Cale. Pirroni had taped the presenter's mouth shut, made him put on the flying doctor uniform and attached the empty pistol to his hand. He had removed Jonny's boot and sock and burned the sole of his foot with a cigarette. Jonny's screams had come through the tape. It had sounded like a brutal act being committed a long way away. Alex's blood had run cold.

The real Pirroni was at the back, following Sarah Compton. He also wore a ski mask, and a long coat. Under the coat was his Colt Commando rifle. The hostages picked their way in single file between the trees. Alex trod carefully. His senses were muffled by the ski mask that covered his ears and it disorientated him. Ahead was a large painted shape visible through the trees. He came into the clearing and saw the white and blue fuselage of a seaplane, moving gently like a yacht in a breeze. A Cessna TU206-G.

The cockpit was empty. The keys were on the seat, as Pirroni had demanded. The back door was open. Instead of seats in the back it had two long bunks with storage underneath, separated by a central gangway. The hostages climbed in, squashing into a line. This was where they no longer knew what to do.

Li was not quite sure what to do either. She had slept in the storage locker underneath the bunk. As soon as she heard voices, she shut the lid and listened to see what would happen.

Pirroni stepped in and moved away from the door. He shrugged off the long coat and hoisted his rifle up so that it lay along his forearm, his hand on the grip and his finger on the trigger.

All the hostages froze. Every eye was on the black metal stock, the chunky magazine and the thick barrel. Alex's mouth went dry. He swallowed and the tape chafed against his lips.

Pirroni sat down on one of the bunks. Alex realized that this gave him cover from any snipers that might be outside. The rifle pointed up at Zoe. She jumped as though it had touched her. Pirroni looked her in the eye and said, 'Out.'

Zoe's eyes widened behind the mask as though she could barely understand the word.

Alex felt light-headed with relief. Could they be getting out at last? He wanted to smile but the tape kept his lips firmly in place. It wasn't over yet.

Another hostage was asked to leave, then another. Pirroni gave Sarah the nod and she climbed out to freedom. Holly was getting ready to go. Pirroni said, 'Stop.'

Alex saw Holly's frightened eyes dancing in the

ski mask. The only hostages still in the plane were them and Jonny Cale.

Pirroni looked at Holly. 'Sit down.' He indicated the seat beside the pilot's in the front.

Holly's hands shook as she reached for the seats and pulled herself between the gap. Awkwardly she manoeuvred herself into the seat.

Pirroni took the phone out of his shirt pocket. He pressed redial. The negotiator answered. 'I am ready to go,' he said. 'I will take two hostages. They will be released when I reach my destination and am safely on my way.'

Alex looked at Jonny. Two hostages were staying? Holly was already chosen. Who else would have to stay? And what would happen to the other one?

Pirroni threw the phone out of the open back door. He took Jonny by the arm, stripped the tape off his hand and removed the pistol, and pushed him after the phone. He slid the door shut.

Amber had her hands in front of her mouth in a frozen gasp of horror.

'Alex is still in there,' said Hex.

'*Dios*,' swore Paulo softly.

The snipers' radio came through. 'Still two hostages on board. Hold your fire.'

Paulo opened the doors of the ambulance and jumped out. Amber and Hex sprang after him. Together they ran down the road and skidded to a halt at the end of the lake. The plane glided towards them down the water. Its nose lifted and it took off into the clear blue sky. On the belly of the plane was a giant black X. Amber remembered Sergeant Powell asking for the plane to be marked. She wondered if they would ever see it again.

15
MISSING

'We're doing our best to find Alex.' Sergeant Powell was briefing Hex, Amber and Paulo in the lorry while Murphy listened to tapes of Pirroni's conversations with the negotiator, looking for clues.

The sergeant had seen enough by now to know that Alpha Force were not just ordinary kids. He talked freely. 'We have a GPS in the plane transmitting Pirroni's position. We're alerting squads on the ground all along his route. When he lands we'll take him. My men will debrief the hostages to see if he hinted at his plans. The police are searching the control room. Pirroni can't go for more than about a thousand kilometres in that plane without refuelling, so he can't leave the country. He may be aiming to meet someone.'

Murphy took off his headphones.

'Anything?' said Sergeant Powell.

Murphy shook his head. 'Innocent conversations about water supplies and whether everyone was in good health. He kept his cards close to his chest.'

'By the way,' said Paulo. 'Wasn't Li in here?'

'Li?' Sergeant Powell shook his head. 'I haven't seen her since last night.'

Amber got up. 'Come on, you guys, let's get a coffee.' She opened the door.

Once they were all out, Amber put her hands on her hips and frowned. 'Does anyone else think it's rather odd that we haven't seen Li?'

Paulo's face was grave. 'I think it's time for a search party. She could be hurt somewhere.'

Hex took out his palmtop. 'We need to do this systematically. I'll get a map . . .' His fingers clicked on the keys.

Amber peered at the screen. 'Seems a little slow.'

Hex's face twitched. 'Every time I did a GPS fix it gobbled up a lot of power. Normal service will be resumed as soon as . . . I hope.' He drummed his fingers on the case impatiently as the screen loaded. 'Right, here we are.' He turned the screen so the others could see. 'This is the camp, this is the lake. If we take a third of the area each, and meet back here . . .'

'You can take off your masks.' Pirroni sat impassively, two guns in his lap. He had reloaded the pistol straight after take-off. Holly was in the front seat beside him and Alex was behind on one of the sideways-facing bunk seats.

Alex took off the ski mask. He peeled up the edges of the sticky tape with his fingernails. It stung. He took a deep breath and pulled hard. He was left holding the limp piece of tape, his eyes watering. Well, at least he might not need to shave for a while.

They were surrounded with bright light. Alex looked out of the window and down. There was nothing but the deep green of the tree canopy. He had an idea that it might be useful to locate the compass in the instrument panel, but there were so many dials – he would need more than a mere glance to spot it. He certainly didn't want to be caught peering at the controls.

Instead he looked for the position of the sun. They seemed to be heading north-west. Where would that take them? The coast? Did Pirroni intend to fly out of Australia in this plane? They would surely have to refuel.

Where would he and Holly end up?

Alex looked around the cabin. He hardly saw it; instead he kept replaying the moment in the control room when Pirroni burned the sole of Jonny Cale's foot. He saw Pirroni grasp Jonny's ankle; saw the cigarette touch the pink flesh; saw Jonny struggle and kick. He heard the chair scuff the floor as Jonny jerked, and his muffled cries behind the duct tape. He saw the concentrated but calm expression on Pirroni's face.

He and Holly were at the mercy of a cold-blooded terrorist.

From her hiding place under the bunk Li could hear intermittent words above the roar of the engine. She realized that Pirroni had kept Alex and a girl with him on the plane. She sighed. Alex was sitting on top of her locker, so she couldn't even peek out. She didn't dare try to attract his attention – Pirroni might spot him looking and then . . . She prepared herself for a long wait.

Hex trudged back, mystified. He had searched his patch and drawn a blank. Maybe Amber and Paulo would find her. He was getting rather worried.

He passed Sergeant Powell, who was wearing an earpiece. 'Hex, I can get one of the police officers to take you back into town soon. They're taking the first of the hostages.'

Hex nodded. 'Er yeah, thanks. We're just waiting for a friend and then . . .'

Sergeant Powell sounded upbeat. 'The GPS is still signalling. We've followed them to North Queensland.' His earpiece made a rasping sound, demanding his attention. He listened. His mood changed. He turned and left without speaking.

Hex was worried. If the others didn't find Li,

the only place to search was the lake— No, the others would find her.

He stopped at the bridge and looked out. The far end of the lake, he realized, was where Amber had played the crocodile game. Could there still be crocodiles around after all the activity with the plane? Someone could vanish in there very easily. He took a swig of water from his bottle and it seemed suddenly very, very cold.

Hex started to search the edge of the lake. Most of it was grass, but then he came across a muddy area close to the bridge. He made out fresh footprints. He knelt down to examine them.

Paulo and Amber saw Hex on the bridge and sprinted towards him, shouting his name.

Hex stood up rapidly. 'Have you found her?' he asked, hope shining in his eyes.

Amber shook her head. She didn't like the way Hex's face fell.

'Then I think I have,' said Hex quietly.

Amber and Paulo followed his gaze down. There were several footprints in the mud by the bridge, but one of them was distinct and small.

'Let's see if that's her size,' said Amber. Slowly and carefully, she placed her own foot beside the print as a comparison. She nodded. 'That's her. She's a size smaller than me.'

Hex said quietly, 'Remember that crocodile?'

The look on Amber's face said that she did; only too well.

Paulo spoke rapidly. 'Listen, *amigos*. Li cannot have been taken by a crocodile. She was aware they were in the lake and she knows better than anyone how they hunt. She would not get close enough to the edge to be in danger.' He took a step backwards. 'If she had been taken by a croc, there would be signs of a struggle. Skid marks.'

'Good point,' said Hex, and began to scan the bank.

For a few minutes they searched in silence. Amber was the first to speak. 'I can't see anything that looks like that.'

'There aren't any more of her footprints either,' said Hex. 'There's only the one here by the bridge.'

They regrouped and looked down at it again.

'Is that definitely her?' said Hex.

Amber nodded. Her voice was quiet. 'I know her

Hi-Tecs. She made me try them on when I lost my boot in the water. That's her.'

'The print is facing into the water,' said Paulo. 'It's as if she got into a boat.'

'A boat?' repeated Hex.

'The plane!' Amber looked at them in excitement. 'It was tethered here when I got up this morning.'

'Why would she have got on the plane?' said Paulo.

'We've looked everywhere else,' said Amber. 'There's nowhere else she could be.'

'But surely she would have told us where she was going,' said Paulo. 'Wouldn't she . . . ?'

16
PURSUIT

Li had been asleep. Gradually, she became aware of the sounds and sensations. Then she remembered. She tried to raise the lid again, but Alex was still sitting on it. She attempted to stretch her cramped limbs, wiggling her toes to keep her circulation going. She wondered how long she would have to stayed curled up in this coffin-like box.

In the cabin, Pirroni put the craft on autopilot and took Alex's knife out of its sheath. They had been flying for an hour over the rainforest of Queensland, heading north.

Alex stiffened. Holly stared at the knife. Alex put a hand on her shoulder and squeezed gently to reassure her.

Pirroni glanced at them and Holly flinched from his look. Alex focused on the instrument panel. To his right, in the centre, was a column of slide-in units. To Alex they looked like car radios. Red lights winked on and off in various configurations. Pirroni selected one of the units and used the tip of the knife to undo some screws. Alex glared as his cherished knife was used for such a crude task but Pirroni was careful. He too knew to take care of a good blade. He slipped the knife down the side of the unit and then pulled out the box.

The unit had a small LCD screen that showed a map – Alex guessed it was the GPS. A bundle of wires streamed out of the back. Pirroni put the blade under them and cut them in one swift move. Cupping his hands, he collected the screws and put them in his pocket. Then he opened the window and dropped the unit into the jungle below.

Pirroni switched the autopilot off and took the plane around in a wide loop. When the plane straightened out he put the autopilot back on again and sat back.

Alex estimated that they were now going south again. Was Pirroni taking them back the way they had come? Why? He knew he would be followed, that's why. He flew away from where he really intended to go and dumped the GPS. Then he turned the craft around. Meanwhile, the SAS would see the signal was no longer moving and be searching for them, thinking they had landed or perhaps crashed. They would be slowed down by the thick jungle too. It was a good plan.

Now, though, he must be setting out for his real destination.

Hex, Amber and Paulo were sitting by the edge of the lake. Shock was etched into their features. They had just heard the news from Sergeant Powell: the GPS signal from the seaplane had suddenly stopped transmitting. They were sending special forces to investigate but it was likely that the plane had crashed.

'I hope we're wrong; I hope Li isn't on that plane.' Paulo's voice was grave. 'And Alex . . .'

There was nothing anyone could say. They watched as the freed hostages walked slowly and quietly towards two police cars to be taken back to their parents.

'Can't be the first time celebrity children have been taken home in a police car,' said Hex.

'They look so dazed,' said Amber. 'It's as if we're the only people left who are still worried.'

'Do you think they have heard about the plane going down?' asked Paulo.

Hex shook his head. 'I don't think the SAS are saying anything about that.'

Two lorries rumbled past. One had been the monitoring room; one had been Sergeant Powell's room.

Sergeant Powell strode up to them, his face grave. 'I need to clear the area,' he said. 'We're moving the operation to North Queensland, where the last trace was seen.'

Amber and Paulo looked tense. Hex looked grim.

Sergeant Powell added, 'This is still a live operation, with people to be rescued. If you don't hear from us within twenty-four hours call me.' He held out a card. Amber took it. 'Now,' he continued, 'we have a problem getting you out of here. The police are taking the hostages home, and we're all heading north. You can wait an hour for a police driver or there's a spare vehicle . . .' He looked at Paulo. 'Are you old enough to drive?'

Paulo drove. Sergeant Powell had given them the field ambulance. They were to take it to the hotel, then call the military to pick it up.

'It's not quite the style we've become accustomed to,' said Hex. The thrill of the 5.7-litre Holdens was still clear in his head. The ambulance window was open and he had to shout to be heard above the noise. 'Can't it do more than 120 kilometres per hour?'

'I am doing my best,' said Paulo. 'My foot is flat on the floor.'

They skirted the edge of the rainforest. The lush greenery gave way to open pasture. On one side was the entrance to a ranch. Sometimes the grass cover was worn away to show a red streak of topsoil. Yellow diamond-shaped signs warned motorists to watch out for kangaroos and camels.

Amber, seated by the window, grabbed Hex's arm. 'Hey, there's a plane.' She craned out of the window, looking up. A light plane flew over, quite low, its undercarriage barely clearing the trees. She drew her head back in. 'No, it's too small and it hasn't got that X on the belly.'

'But why would Pirroni come back here anyway?' said Hex.

Amber shrugged. 'I guess he wouldn't. Can't help looking, though.' She rested her hand along the door and drummed her fingers.

Another yellow diamond-shaped sign went by: ROAD TRAINS NEXT 900KM.

'Hey, we might see a road train!' exclaimed Hex.

'What's that?' asked Amber.

'It's like a convoy of lorries, lashed together and pulled by a great big engine at the front,' Paulo replied.

Hex was talking fast. 'They travel at nearly a hundred and thirty kilometres per hour and stop for nothing. They're so wide they take up the whole road. If we meet one, we have to get off the road out of its way.' His eyes were glittering and he took a breath to say more, but Amber's face stopped him. 'What's the matter?' he said.

Amber's expression was pure disdain. 'You guys.'

'But Amber, they've got ninety-eight wheels,' said Paulo with feeling. 'Imagine that.'

Amber folded her arms. 'So?'

'You must have them in the States,' said Hex.

'If we do,' drawled Amber, 'I ain't interested.'

'How can you be so soulless?' said Hex. 'They've got ninety-eight wheels.'

They came to a turning by a sign for a roadhouse. Paulo slowed momentarily and swung the ambulance onto it.

'This isn't the way back,' said Hex.

'No,' said Paulo. 'But look over there.' He pointed in the direction they had been travelling.

Hex and Amber looked. There was a cloud of dust in the distance, rolling along the ground as though the sand was boiling.

'There's a dust storm over there,' explained Paulo. 'So wherever Pirroni's going, it won't be that way.'

'But he's gone north,' said Amber. 'He's not going to be down here anyway.'

'Just a hunch.' Paulo grinned. 'And there was a sign for a roadhouse. We need diesel.'

A short while later they pulled up at the roadhouse. It was just a shack in a section of scrubby pasture. On one of the fields behind it was the plane that had flown over them earlier. The pilot was refuelling it from a pump in the corner of the field. He finished, reholstered the nozzle and ambled towards the roadhouse, adjusting his bush hat against the glare of the sun.

'How's that for outback facilities?' said Amber. 'How many of the locals have planes out here?'

'Quite a lot,' replied Paulo. 'The ranches here use planes to round up cattle.' He steered the ambulance towards a diesel pump, braked and cut the engine. 'They're so huge, there's no other way of getting around them.' He jumped out. Hex and Amber followed.

'Another plane,' said Amber, tilting her head back to look. 'By the time we get to town I'm gonna be a nervous . . .' Her voice tailed off. She squinted into the sky. 'Was that . . . ?'

Hex was looking up too. 'X marks the spot.'

The plane carried the distinctive mark painted on the belly of the fuselage.

'Phone Sergeant Powell,' said Paulo immediately, sprinting for the roadhouse.

The others crowded in behind him. Inside, it was a big wooden room – a general store combined with a lounge bar. The pilot of the light plane was sitting on a stool at a bar chatting to a deeply tanned woman behind the counter. Their heads were close together over their beers. They looked round sharply at the three figures who had burst in so suddenly.

The woman called out, 'We're closed, mate. Leave the money on the counter.'

'We need to make a phone call, urgently,' said Hex.

'Don't have a public phone,' said the woman. The man whispered something to her and she giggled in return. Her leathery skin creased deeply as she smiled.

Amber had the card with Sergeant Powell's number on it. She walked up to the counter, holding it out. 'It's a matter of national security,' she said. 'Didn't you see on TV about the siege?'

'I was watching the rugby,' replied the woman.

'Look, you can phone it yourself if you don't believe us—' Amber got no further.

The man took a deep draught of beer and rounded on her. 'Didn't you hear the lady? She's closed.' His mouth was set in a tight, hostile line. 'Now why don't you pesky kids just go and play your games somewhere else?'

Paulo pulled at Hex's and Amber's sleeves. 'Come on,' he said.

They had barely got outside before Amber exploded. 'What kind of dumb—?'

'Amber, look.' Paulo tapped her arm and pointed in the direction of the light plane standing in the field. 'All refuelled and ready to go.'

They sprinted over to it. 'Hope he left it unlocked,' said Hex.

Paulo pulled the door open and scanned the ignition area. 'Right . . . master switch to turn on the electricity . . .' He flicked a switch. 'Primer . . . to put some fuel into the engine . . .' He pressed another switch. 'But no keys.' He dug under a panel with his fingernails and levered it off. 'We will have to hotwire it to start it.' He reached delicately into the panel and pulled: two wires came out in his fist. Taking one in each hand, he touched them together.

The engine spluttered into life. The propeller started spinning and became a circular blur.

'Hey, guys,' said Amber, looking at the interior, 'this is a cosy two-seater.'

'Can you squash in the back, Amber?' asked Hex.

There was a narrow crack behind the two seats. Amber climbed up and eased herself into it. 'Well, it's hardly what I would call comfortable.'

Hex belted himself into the co-pilot seat. Paulo pulled the door shut and took the parking brake off. The plane began to move. He guided it around in a large arc until it was facing straight down the runway, then opened the throttle. The plane rumbled down the field.

Hex looked at Paulo, worried. 'Can we get into the air with Amber's weight?'

Amber cuffed Hex around the head. 'Wash your mouth out.'

'We can carry an extra passenger if we take a

longer run to take off,' said Paulo. 'Amber, how many hot dogs did you eat?'

'Mind your own business,' she said. 'You're lucky you don't have to take my luggage as well. Anyway, I never knew you could fly a plane, Paulo.' She shifted her position. Already she was getting cramp.

'I hope he flies them better than helicopters,' said Hex, remembering a rather wobbly experience in Canada when Paulo took the controls of a chopper.

'Planes are much easier than helicopters,' answered Paulo. 'My uncle used to visit our ranch in a Cessna and he taught me.' He felt the nose lift. 'Ah, here we go.' He eased the plane off the ground.

Hex checked off the instruments. The plane was rather basic compared with the flight simulators he was used to. 'We have airspeed indicator, artificial horizon, turn co-ordinator, altimeter, vertical speed indicator . . . . Oh.' He peered into a hole in front of him. 'We have a couple of wires where the radio should be. Great.' He took out his palmtop and powered it up.

'Pirroni was heading south-south-east,' said

Amber. 'He must have dumped the GPS and doubled back.' She craned her neck to look at the tiny screen.

Hex frowned at his palmtop. 'This is nearly out of batteries. I can get one more fix, which will show us an immediate map, and we can plot a course that's on Pirroni's trail.'

The palmtop showed they were heading well away from the Daintree Rainforest. Hex indicated a line with his finger. 'He could be going for this point on the coast here. We'd better keep a close eye on the ground in case he lands.'

'At least in this open space we should be able to see,' said Amber.

Down below, the colour of the land changed. The lush green of the rainforest dried out and the ground became deep orange, like the surface of Mars. A gravelly strip marked the only road for miles, a long stripe of deserted hardtop. Occasionally they passed over a vehicle: sometimes it was a truck, tiny from that distance; sometimes it was a road train. Now and then there was a wreck – burnt out near a scrubby wood, or simply abandoned and thickly coated with dust, as if it was being absorbed into the red earth. But mostly they saw no sign of life below them. Amber, Hex and Paulo were venturing into the most arid, hostile place in the giant land of Australia, a land of frequent storms and ferocious fires – the Red Centre.

17
RED CENTRE

'Paulo, look at that.' Hex pointed through the cockpit window at a smudge on the skyline. It was a line of dust a few miles in front of the plane.

'It could be that storm,' said Amber.

'Better steer around it,' said Paulo. 'Storms are not good news.'

As he began to turn, the windscreen clouded over and the plane dropped like a stone.

'Aaagh, Paulo!' screamed Amber. She gripped the back of his seat so hard her fingers hurt. Hex clung onto the door, his arm rigid.

Paulo wrestled with the throttle, his teeth gritted. He pulled back on the control wheel to try to gain more height.

The windscreen cleared. The plane stopped its rapid descent. It flew along, bumping like a boat caught on choppy water.

'Well done, Paulo,' said Hex. 'Forwards good, downwards not.'

Amber adjusted her uncomfortable position. 'Paulo, I nearly lost my breakfast. And that's not funny because if I do I shall have to find some more.'

Before Paulo could reply it happened again.

The windscreen went completely dark. The plane dropped. It was like being in an elevator plummeting to the ground. It lifted Hex and Paulo from their seats and pressed the seatbelts painfully into their legs. It threw Amber hard against the ceiling.

Paulo's stomach was in his mouth. He jerked on the throttle. He had to gain height. He couldn't see anything out of the windscreen. The altimeter reading was the only information he could take in. It seesawed crazily.

They hit a clear patch. They could see again, but without the drag of all the dust the plane soared into the sky. Within moments it was vertical. Paulo scarcely knew what he was doing, but he guided it round in a smooth loop until it was horizontal again. Then they continued as though nothing had happened.

'Paulo,' said Hex gravely, 'we have just looped the loop. Whenever I do that in a flight simulator, I crash.'

'I think that was pretty cool,' said Paulo. But his voice came out as a rasp and he looked bug-eyed.

'Paulo,' grumbled Amber, 'if we crash, I shall eat you. And I won't necessarily wait until you're dead.'

Paulo saw red earth whirling towards the windscreen like a blizzard. 'Here it comes again.' He braced himself against the controls.

The plane plummeted again. Hex and Amber clung on, their knuckles white. Paulo desperately worked the throttle. He noticed to his horror that the altimeter was in the red zone. There was a bang. He hoped it was the wheels hitting the tops of some trees and not the ground.

The engine started to splutter. Paulo went cold. Sand had worked into the filters and was interfering with the air intake. The engine could stall.

They had to land, but they were going far too fast and if they touched down at this speed they would crash. He had to reduce airspeed drastically. Paulo pulled all the flaps out.

The engine coughed and misfired. 'Come on,' Paulo found himself shouting, 'come on.' The dust cleared and the plane soared giddily at forty-five degrees.

'Paulo, look, there's a road.' Amber got a perfect view of a black strip of tarmac ahead of them. 'Please tell me we're not going to land upside down.'

Paulo tried to level the plane. It dropped again and knocked all the air out of him like a punch. There was a bump as the wheels touched down. But the plane bounced upwards again.

'More flaps, Paulo,' yelled Hex.

'They're all the way,' Paulo shouted back. The plane touched down again and hopped into the air. The engine coughed and died. Paulo put the nose downwards and this time when the tyres bit the road, the plane stayed on the ground. Paulo braked hard. The craft skidded and he eased off. Little by little he brought it to a standstill.

He sank back in his seat. His hands flopped away from the controls and he let out a long sigh. Amber patted him on the shoulder, shaking her head. She was speechless.

Hex looked out of the window. All around the dust was swirling, turning the sky a thick red. The wind roared, steadied, then roared again.

The plane began to move.

'OK, Paulo, that's enough,' said Amber weakly.

'I didn't touch anything,' said Paulo. 'We shouldn't be moving.' The plane drifted along the road and started to pick up speed.

'Well, do something!' exclaimed Amber.

Paulo had his hands back on the controls and his feet on the rudder pedals, but the plane was being swept along by the wind. He put the parking brake on, but that was worse. It skidded on the locked wheels and when he released it again they were going even faster.

'Look at that wind speed,' said Hex. 'Sixty-four kilometres per hour.'

'We're being blown like a yacht,' said Amber. 'Try pulling the flaps in.'

'I have. It's not doing anything.'

The dust settled again and the plane slowed. 'What's that in the distance?' said Hex.

Amber peered into the russet gloom. 'Lights. Could it be a roadhouse? There aren't any towns out here.'

Another curtain of dust erased the lights. The plane surged forwards again. When the dust cloud had passed, the lights were bigger.

'We're getting closer,' said Amber.

'How do you suppose we'll stop this thing?' asked Hex.

'I think we just go with the flow and wait for the storm to die down,' said Amber. 'So long as nothing comes . . . at least we're sheltered.'

Another wave of dust passed, thick like soup. It cleared.

'Those lights are closer still,' said Paulo.

Hex squinted at them. 'I think they're moving as well . . . towards us.'

Paulo and Amber stared into the distance.

'You're right,' said Paulo.

'But what is it?' asked Amber.

'*Dios*,' whispered Paulo.

Amber realized there was something around the lights. They took shape to become two headlights, with a gigantic fender like a snowplough, and a smaller cab. A string of orange lights like carnival decorations looped across the top.

Hex said, 'It's the road train.'

'Well, you were so keen to see it,' said Amber. Her throat strangled the words so they came out without the bravado she'd tried for.

Paulo wrestled to regain control of the plane. Instead he spun it in a circle. When the wind eased they heard the roar of the road train's colossal tyres and the rattle and clatter as its great loaded axles bounced over potholes. It was approaching fast.

'It's too close,' yelled Amber.

Paulo pulled at the door handle. 'Get out, quick!' He dived out.

Hex followed, then Amber. They landed hard and tumbled off the blacktop into the scrubby bush.

Hex was the first to get to his feet. 'Run!' he yelled.

The wind threw red dust in their eyes, up their noses, into their ears. It scoured their faces, necks and hands. It stung like acid. Amber stumbled blindly, one hand protecting her eyes and the other feeling in front of her as if she was playing blind man's buff. Paulo took her hand and led her. She followed, placing complete trust in him.

Over the roaring wind they heard a loud, blaring air horn, like the kind used on big locomotives in America. Amber opened her eyes.

In the split second before she closed them again, she saw the road train boom down the highway, into the little Cessna. The plane slipped under the engine's front wheels before the lorry's momentum batted it aside. The road train rumbled on, its sides festooned with orange running lights like a travelling fair. The wind howled again and the sky rained needles. The three huddled together in a tight ball, hiding their faces in their clothes.

Pirroni struggled to land. The world outside had turned to brick-red soup. Gusts of wind flung the plane back into the air whenever the wheels on the underside of the floats touched down. Alex watched Pirroni wrestle with the controls, grim-faced. The terrorist's expression was that of a man who expected to win because he would battle for the longest.

Finally the elements gave in. The plane stayed on terra firma. When the windscreen cleared, a tree loomed directly ahead, too close to avoid. Pirroni cut the engine but the propeller carved into a heavy branch. The blades sheared off with a screaming sound and the cabin lurched violently. The wind picked up again and reclaimed control of the craft. Pirroni pulled the plane round in a circle. Gradually it slowed and finally stopped.

The wind howled around the cabin. Pirroni unbuckled his seatbelt and checked his gun.

Holly turned to look at Alex. She was clearly terrified. 'Have we crashed?' she whispered.

'We'll be OK,' he said softly. Inside he didn't feel as confident. The plane was damaged and they were in the middle of a dust storm. What would happen now?

In the bunk, Li waited. Her ears strained for the sound of voices. She heard none. She knew they were on the ground – she had felt every bump as the plane circled on the rough scrubland. She had felt the lurch as the propeller smashed into the tree. But now there was silence.

Should she move? Were the others still conscious? Should she lift the bunk lid and look?

A smell wafted into the tiny space. It was cigarette smoke. Alex didn't smoke; Pirroni must still be alive and in control of the plane.

Li resigned herself to staying put for a while longer.

The storm passed. Amber risked opening her eyes, shielding them with her fingers just in case. She saw bright sunshine, clear and dust free, the surface of the red earth smoothed as though by a giant hand. The trees were still.

They were all coated with the red dust. It stuck to the sweat on their faces and clothes like a fuzz of velvet. Their eyes and teeth showed brilliant white in contrast.

The black scarf Amber wore around her neck felt tight and claustrophobic in the heat. She loosened it. 'Guys,' she said, 'do I look as red and fuzzy as you?'

Hex opened his mouth to speak and spluttered instead. He looked past her. 'Oh my God – the plane.'

It lay by the side of the carriageway. One wing was buckled and the fuselage was creased like an empty drinks can.

Amber swore. 'Those road trains have ninety-eight wheels, huh?'

'They can weigh ninety tonnes,' said Hex. 'In case you were interested.'

'I am so not impressed,' said Amber.

'Come on,' said Paulo. 'Let's check the damage.'

They walked towards the plane. Now that the air was no longer murky with dust the full heat of the sun beat down on them. 'We need something to cover ourselves with,' said Hex, squinting up at the sky.

'This does not look good,' said Paulo when they got up close.

The plane lay on its side, the roof and door crumpled, as if it had been folded. One window remained, its surface white and frosted. Hex ran his finger over it. 'It's been sandblasted. Literally.'

Amber lay on the fuselage on her tummy and tried to reach into the plane. The doorway was a narrow crevice. 'I can't even get my shoulders in,' she gasped. She straightened up. 'No chance of using it as a shelter.'

'Are there any blankets or anything in the back?' asked Paulo.

'There was nothing,' said Amber. She rubbed a bruise on her hip. 'Not even a carpet. I was sitting on bare metal.'

'There are two water bottles.' Hex managed to hook them out and passed one each to Paulo and Amber. 'That's all there is. There's a first-aid kit but it's jammed under the seat.'

Leaning against the plane, Hex pulled his palmtop out of its carrying case and switched it on.

'So where are we?' said Paulo, peering at the screen.

The screen remained blank. 'Who knows?' said Hex. 'The batteries are dead. I could try recharging it from the plane – if I could get at the battery.' He looked at the crumpled fuselage and let out a sigh.

'We can take the compass out of the dashboard,' said Amber. Hex gave her an odd look. 'Or whatever it's called in a plane,' she grumbled. 'I don't know – it looks like a dashboard to me.'

But Hex was not looking at her; he was looking past her.

Amber was about to follow his gaze when a quiet voice said, 'Your compass is not reliable here.'

They turned. A brooding face of leathery black skin regarded them. The scorching sun overhead cast dark shadows on his brows, making his eye sockets deep pits.

'The iron in the rocks will affect your compass,' he said. 'You need to navigate by the sun and stars.'

Hex tried to guess the age of the Aboriginal in front of him. The face was creased and lined, but the hair was jet-black and thickly waved without even a trace of grey. He wore jeans and a checked shirt open to the navel with the sleeves ripped out. His feet were bare, the toenails long and curved over like claws.

Amber knew there were often tensions between the Aboriginals and the settlers who had come later to Australia. It was similar with the American Indians. Would this local be friendly to some stranded westerners, or hostile? She wasn't too sure about the way this man was eyeing Hex's palmtop.

The man spoke again. 'I need your help,' he said.

18
One False Move

Alex was drenched in sweat; they all were. The inside of the plane was as hot as a greenhouse. Outside, the storm still howled and flung earth at the plane. But Pirroni sat calmly.

Alex marvelled at the terrorist's focus and determination. He never lost sight of his goal. If something went wrong he either sorted it out, or he waited for conditions that were more favourable. While they were waiting, Pirroni had drunk water and smoked one cigarette; those were the only things Alex had seen him do. Otherwise he seemed like a machine. The man had the focus of an assassin.

Not for the first time, Alex thought about his knife. Its theft was like an insult that kept stinging. He didn't know how he was going to get it back, but he would. Then he pulled himself up. He must keep calm. The mission came first.

At last the air cleared and Alex, Pirroni and Holly could see where they were. It looked like a parched forest in a Martian landscape. Brushwood in a desiccated green grew in clumps on the red soil. Termite mounds rose in irregular towers. To one side was the tree they had hit, on the edge of a shrivelled wood.

Pirroni lifted the gun from his lap and pointed it at Holly. 'Take your seatbelt off, open the door and get out.'

Holly fumbled with the belt but managed to unfasten it. She fumbled with the door handle too, before jumping out.

Pirroni turned to Alex. 'Now you.'

Alex did as he was instructed and landed on the red soil next to Holly.

Pirroni climbed out, carrying his holdall. Alex could see the outline of the Colt Commando rifle and the water bottles.

Of course, thought Alex. He wants to get as far away from the plane as possible. If they stayed there, anyone searching from the air would spot them in no time. 'Wait,' he said. 'We need water too.' He looked at Pirroni.

Under the bunk, Li waited, listening. She heard three people get out of the plane. Now one climbed back in – probably male from the weight of the footsteps. He went into the cockpit.

Then he came nearer, clambering through to the back and standing right beside her hiding place. She heard a cupboard being opened, then closed. She heard the opposite bunk lid being opened.

Li breathed very slowly and deeply. She couldn't hold her breath, because if she needed to spring out and fight for her life, her muscles wouldn't be oxygenated enough and she would tire quickly. So she took in as much air as she could as silently as possible.

If it was Pirroni, he would probably have a gun,

so all she could hope for was that the element of surprise would work in her favour.

The crack where the lid met the side of the bunk widened and light poured in. She tensed like a cobra, ready to strike. A large shadow was visible. The lid was raised further. The shadow adjusted its position and an arm reached in.

Li recognized the two watches just in time. The next thing she saw was Alex's face, sideways on and very, very surprised.

Their eyes met for just a moment. Li put as much warning into her expression as she could manage, then lowered her head. Her hair spilled over her face in an inky veil and she melted back into the shadowed interior of the bunk.

Alex stood holding the bunk open. He felt like his brain had been scrambled. Li! What was she doing here? *Think*, he told himself. The important thing is not to give her away. Behave as though the bunk had nothing in it. He lowered the lid and opened a cupboard, deliberately paying the bunk no more attention. He was looking for something to carry the water bottles in. Concentrate on that, he told himself. Look for a bag, just as you were doing a moment ago, before you saw Li.

He found one and put the water bottles in it. He left some for Li, out of sight. There was a medical kit and he left that for her too. Then he got out of the plane.

'Quickly,' said Pirroni. He indicated that Alex and Holly should walk into the wood.

Alex took Holly's hand and began to walk. He didn't want to leave Li all alone in the wilderness. What would she do? But for all their sakes he had to act as if she wasn't there at all.

Li waited until she could hear no more footsteps, then opened the lid a fraction. There was no-one in sight. She opened it fully, still prepared to defend herself, then stood up cautiously.

She was alone.

She stepped out of the bunk and massaged some life back into her cramped limbs. But every moment she spent doing that was a moment when Pirroni and his hostages were getting further away. She had to get going. Her own survival, as well as Alex's, depended on it.

But first she knelt in the doorway and studied the ground for footprints. The ground was baked hard like terracotta and nothing showed. She got out carefully and moved away from the plane a little. Then it hit her. Not only was she alone; she was alone in a great wide sun-cracked earthbowl miles from anywhere. The blue sky above her seemed immense. She felt vulnerable and insignificant, like an ant.

Calm down, she told herself. You're not alone, you're following Pirroni. What would he do? He would get into the wood as soon as possible. She moved to the edge of the trees.

And there she had her proof: a footprint in a shallow gully where the soil was softer because it was sheltered from the sun. It looked like the Timberlands Alex wore.

Li smiled. Alex was leaving her a trail. They were in this together.

She hopped back into the plane to look for materials she could take. She searched the aircraft and found water bottles and a medical kit. She couldn't take all the medical kit because it was too big, but she packed the most useful items into a tool bag – taking scissors, antiseptic cream, sutures and needles and strong bandages that could double as ropes.

In the bunk was the blanket she had rested on for all that time. She pulled it out. It was bright blue. She dragged it outside and laid it on the ground. It made a stark contrast to the rusty earth. Unravelling her tool bag, Li took out the medical kit scissors and cut the blanket into three strips. Then she arranged them to form a giant arrow next to the plane, weighted down with stones and pointing in the direction she intended to take through the trees. If anyone flew over and saw the wreck, they would know there were survivors to find.

She began to walk into the wood. The air smelled astringent, of eucalyptus. She looked back at the plane for a moment. Leaving it went against all her survival instincts; you didn't leave your vehicle when you were marooned in a hostile environment. She made a cut in the tree with scissors and hoped someone would find it.

* * *

Tommy Bininuwuy stopped his pick-up truck. 'We're here,' he said.

It hadn't taken Amber, Paulo and Hex long to decide they should go with Tommy. For now, they had little idea where Pirroni was, and they couldn't carry on searching without transport. This way, if they helped Tommy, they could stock up on supplies and figure out a way to get back on the trail. They might even be able to borrow a vehicle.

They looked out through the dusty windows at the settlement. A cluster of around twenty homes stood among the sparse trees; they were made from concrete breeze blocks and roofed with corrugated iron. Chickens ran between the houses. A radio provided a quiet, tinny accompaniment to their squawking. A woman sat on the veranda of the nearest home. She looked up from her sewing and waved as she saw the truck. Two other Aboriginals drawing designs on flattened pieces of eucalyptus bark checked out the new arrivals, pausing with their brushes poised over a jam-jar full of paint-cloudy water. All the people shared the same jet-black skin and profuse curls that Tommy had.

Amber, Paulo and Hex jumped down from the truck. Tommy led them onto the veranda past a woman in a blue T-shirt with large pink flowers who was bending over and talking to a little girl. Amber looked down to smile a greeting. Both the woman and the child ignored her.

Amber was taken aback. They had looked right through her as though she wasn't there.

Inside the building was a schoolroom painted pale yellow. A line of wooden tables with chairs faced a blackboard.

Tommy had not explained to them what he needed them to help with, but when they saw the front bench it was obvious. On it, in pieces, was a computer. Monitor and keyboard were intact, but the cover had been removed from the central processing unit and its green circuit boards lay exposed.

Amber laughed out loud. 'Hex – all yours!'

Hex was already peering into the open machine. 'Fantastic!' he exclaimed, his eyes gleaming with delight. 'I haven't seen a Pentium for years! How did it go wrong exactly?'

* * *

Pirroni walked slowly. Deeper into the wood, the ground was rutted. Some of the tree trunks were scorched. Ashy deposits carpeted the floor. On top of them, eucalyptus leaves were scattered like tiny scimitars. From time to time the trees thinned out and gave way to termite mounds. But this time they were not the red, bulbous mounds they had seen before. These were pale, slender wafers, set out at intervals in the clearing like ghostly tombstones. Despite the trees there was little shade; the air was suffocating and stale.

Alex noticed that Pirroni was now walking heavily. Could it be because of his lameness? A bright-green snake slithered away from under his feet and he realized the terrorist was doing it deliberately to make sure that any wildlife heard the vibrations and fled.

Alex scraped the black forest floor aside with his toe and found the red earth beneath. To delay a little longer, he tripped.

Pirroni turned round and looked at him coldly. 'If you injure yourself I will leave you.'

Of course. That was why Pirroni was taking them

so slowly. In this desolate place even something as insignificant as a sprain meant a prolonged but certain death.

Alex looked behind him at the place where he had trodden. He was pleased to see the big red streak and a firm print. Then a thought came like a dark cloud and spoiled his optimism: he had been looking forward to building on skills like this in the army. He shook his head. He must keep focused on the mission.

Holly took his hand. She looked up at him and managed a smile. Her face and clothes were red with a fine layer of dust and she looked like part of the landscape. She was being very brave. 'Are you OK without your glasses?' he asked.

'I'm OK. A little short-sighted. Not much. I can get about . . . I know you'll get us through this,' she whispered.

He felt a great wave of protectiveness and squeezed her hand to reassure her. Then he let go, tripped again, leaving another mark, and caught up with her.

Pirroni put his hand up. 'Stop.'

He retraced his steps, looking carefully at the ground. Alex's heart was in his mouth. What if he saw his clue? It was highly visible, a red streak in the black ash, where hardly any other footprints showed. But Pirroni stopped when he found one of his own footprints and knelt down. He reached into his bag and brought out a rifle bullet.

Alex's mouth, already dry from the heat, turned to sandpaper.

Pirroni took out Alex's knife and experimentally scraped at the footprint. It was soft. He chose a spot in the middle where his heel would have been and skewered the knife into the ground up to the hilt, turning it to bore a wide hole. The brutality of the action made Holly wince. Alex felt steel in his soul. You don't do that with my knife, he thought. Somehow, soon, I'll be taking it back from you.

Pirroni put back some of the loose earth to make the hole narrower. He searched in his pocket and took out one of the screws from the plane's GPS unit. He dropped it into the hole, checked to see which way up it had landed and packed the loose earth carefully around it. He dropped the bullet in after it. Then he smoothed the surface over the hole so that the footprint looked intact, and stood up. He drank some water, surveying his booby trap. Then he resumed walking.

Alex was in no doubt how nasty that booby trap was. If someone stepped on the hole – which was likely if they were tracking them and checking the size of the footprint – their weight would push the bullet onto the screw and fire it. The bullet would go straight up into their leg and probably take the limb off.

Before Alex set off, he picked up a twig and silently bent it in two places so that it formed a letter N, meaning negative – one of the international signals for danger. He dropped it behind him, then caught up with Holly.

But his thoughts were somewhere else. Be careful, Li, he said to himself. Be very, very careful.

19
Before the Maelstrom

If Li missed Alex's next mark she could wander for ever. She picked her way carefully, scanning the ground with every step. But she saw nothing. Black ash coated the floor, and its powdery surface hardly took prints at all.

The heat sapped all her energy, making it impossible to walk energetically even if she had wanted to. The air was so warm she could hardly breathe. No matter how deeply she inhaled, it felt as if nothing was going into her lungs. She rationed her water, knowing it might have to last a long time.

But one of the things she had with her was water purification tablets, so if she found another source she would be able to use it.

She had to believe she would see more tracks, but the blank ground was scary. Be logical, she told herself. You're not seeing tracks because Pirroni will be doing his best to cover them. Alex would have to be careful leaving her clues in case Pirroni noticed. She might not see one for a while. She just had to trust that there would be more.

Every so often she used the scissors to cut big arrows into trees. The scorched trunks were particularly good as the wood underneath showed up pale.

Someone else would follow; she told herself that. She had made the plane visible, and people would be looking for Pirroni. Once she started thinking about what she would do if she caught up with Pirroni on her own. She put it swiftly out of her mind. One step at a time, she told herself. Look for Alex's signs. She put all the mental strength she had developed in training into concentrating on her job.

Everywhere there were signs of recent fires: the ashy floor; the scorched trees. Her every footstep crackled as tinder-dry twigs snapped under her. Forest fires were a real possibility here.

She saw a red skid mark with a bootprint. Her spirits lifted; it didn't look accidental. She walked a little further. There was another bootprint, not a Timberland. A twisted twig lay on top of it to form a letter. She avoided stepping on the footprint; the letter N must be a warning. She was relived to see a deliberate sign. As if to comfort her even more, she heard rustling and cawing in the distance. A flock of birds had been disturbed by something large. Her quarry must be quite close. 'Bless you, Alex,' she said softly.

Hex clamped the cover of the PC back on, reconnected the monitor, keyboard and power supply – and switched on. The machine hummed, the hard drive started spinning and the screen flowered into life.

Amber and Paulo were sitting with him at the bench. Paulo looked impressed. 'What was it, Hex?'

'Some of the lovely indigenous wildlife had eaten through one of the IDE cables.'

Paulo looked blank.

'The cable from the motherboard to the hard drive,' Hex explained. 'The computer thought the hard drive was missing. Most PCs have a second cable going to the CD-ROM, so I put the hard drive and CD-ROM onto the same cable, made the CD-ROM the slave device by re-jumpering the device selector and—'

Amber was pulling a face at Paulo. 'Don't you wish you'd never asked?' She took a swig of water. They now had freshly boiled water from the settlement.

Tommy sat at the working computer and beamed. 'It's marvellous,' he said.

Hex concentrated on talking to the more appreciative members of his audience. 'I also changed some more jumpers on the motherboard to overclock the system, so in effect you now have a faster PC. While I'm here I'll just have a look at your setup and data management.' His fingers flew over the keys.

More people had come into the schoolroom, among them the woman in the flowered T-shirt. They crowded around the bench. Hex was clicking through systems boxes on the screen and they exclaimed in amazement, clapping Tommy on the back.

'They seem pleased,' said Paulo.

'Yes, but have you noticed something?' said Amber. 'They're congratulating Tommy. It's as if the three of us are invisible.'

Tommy indicated the three friends. 'These are the people who had helped me make the computer work,' he said.

All of a sudden, the woman in the flowered T-shirt turned and spoke directly to Amber and Paulo. 'Hello, I'm Suzu. The computer is very important to the school. Our children need to know how to survive in a foreign culture.'

Now she was perfectly friendly, thought Amber. That one introduction had changed everything. It was as if we didn't exist until our relationship to them was explained.

Hex finished zapping boxes on the screen. 'I'm just defragmenting your hard drive and removing Findfast, which should make it run even better.' He looked at Suzu. 'How many children use this computer?'

'All the children in this outstation – around thirty.'

Hex goggled. 'Strewth, you need more machines.' He brought out his palmtop, then a small power lead. 'Do you have anywhere I could plug this in?'

Tommy pointed at the device. 'When I saw him with this I thought they could help,' he told Suzu. Hex pointed to a black box on the desk. 'Would you pass that transformer?'

Suzu handed it over. Hex inspected it, tweaked some switches on his palmtop to make it compatible, then switched the machine on. As its screen lit up, he smiled at it like an old friend, then got to work and fired off a few e-mails. First he sent a grid reference to Sergeant Powell and copied it to Amber's uncle. Then he sent a general e-mail to several of his friends: 'Does anyone want a deserving home for an old machine?' Hacker friends who used the latest technology often donated their old computers to local schools or charities.

After a few minutes he looked up from the screen. 'OK. I have three Pentium Pros for you. They can be couriered to anywhere you like.'

A look of deep gratitude spread over Tommy's face. 'And now we must do something for you. I think we might be able to help you find your friends.'

Hex was about to unplug his palmtop, but Amber stopped him. 'Before you shut that down, have you still got the co-ordinates of where we last saw Pirroni's plane?'

Hex flicked the display to a different screen and she picked up a pencil and writing pad that were on the bench and began to scribble.

Suzu bustled off. Tommy said to Paulo, 'I will drive you where you need to go. But first, you must have food.'

Paulo smiled. 'That is very kind; thank you.' He noticed Amber calling up a map on the GPS. 'Amber, what are you doing?'

'This is our current position here. We know where we last spotted Pirroni, and what his bearing was. He'd have had to land too because of the storm, so he can't be that far from where we came down.' She scribbled as she talked, doing the calculations and constructing a diagram with the results. 'We can allow for the storm because we know the wind speed reading was sixty-four k.p.h. . . .' She looked up. 'What speed were we flying at, and what speed do you reckon Pirroni would have been doing in his aircraft?'

Suzu returned with a wooden bowl. Hex's nostrils caught a delicious smell. Then he checked himself. He had heard stories about bush tucker; indeed, some of the games in the TV show involved making contestants eat revolting things.

'Oh wow!' exclaimed Paulo. He looked as though he was about to die of bliss. 'Corned beef hash.'

Amber looked up from her calculations. 'All *riiiiight*,' she grinned as Tommy handed out bowls.

In less than an hour they were ready to set off. Hex and Paulo sat on a striped rug in the back of the Toyota truck. Tommy and Amber were in the front. As they drove out of the camp, several youths carrying flaming torches headed out into the clearing. Their charcoal-coloured limbs resembled slender twigs poking out from the legs of their shorts, which was all they wore.

Amber turned to Tommy. 'What's going on?'

'A fire is coming. We burn the area around the camp to get rid of all the grass and trees. It goes out before the real fire arrives. Then the real fire cannot reach our homes.'

One of the youths touched his flame to a clump of scrubby grass. Tinder-dry, it caught immediately, sending a line of flame along the ground like a burning fuse.

Tommy took them out over the plain. There was no road, only a faint track where other vehicles had passed. Amber spread out her map on the dashboard. The calculations had come easily to her thanks to her experience navigating aboard yachts, and she was confident she had pinpointed a small area where Pirroni was likely to have landed. It was quite close to where they had come down themselves. They would patrol a radius around their own wreck and look for signs of a landing. Even if Pirroni had taken off again, he would not have gone far.

Tommy braked and the truck skidded to a halt. He called over his shoulder to Hex and Paulo, 'You must come and sit in the cab. Another dust storm is coming.'

Hex and Paulo scrambled in, jamming Amber's thigh against the gear lever. As they pulled the door shut, the sky darkened and a thick red haze cloaked the windscreen. Tommy drove on without slowing. He steered as though he could still see. Hex looked back and saw as the dust thinned that the bushman had just piloted them around a tree. He knows every tree and boulder, he thought.

Tommy's face was grim. 'Where the dust storms come, the fire comes too.'

20
Racing the Flames

The dust storm lashed the trees. Alex and Holly huddled together. Pirroni sat hunched by a tree trunk. Alex opened his eyes briefly and couldn't even see his hand. It was like being in a thick fog, but a fog full of nails. He could hear nothing but the wind in his ears. Which way was up? He had no idea. Holly clung to him like a koala; he had to be strong for her. Pirroni was immobilized too but there was no possibility of using this as a chance to get away. The storm blinded and deafened them.

The wind slowed. The quiet came like relief. Tiny

noises seemed magnified. Alex could hear Holly breathing next to him. But it wasn't normal breathing; it was a rasping wheeze. The wind got up again and he still seemed to hear Holly fighting for breath, but that might have been the memory of it preying on his mind. Did she have asthma? If she did and she had a bad attack, she might die.

Another lull came, and this time it lasted. Pirroni got to his feet and Alex helped Holly up. He felt as if he had been spun around in a blindfold. Which direction had they been going in?

A flock of birds rose in a shrieking cloud. Pirroni stopped and looked at them. It seemed to ring some alarm bell in his mind. He turned to look back the way they had come.

Alex turned to look too. Grey smoke hugged the ground and filled in the gaps between the termite mounds. It looked like morning mist on a winter's day – except this was no mist. A smell of burning reached Alex's nostrils.

'Fire!' he yelled.

Pirroni ran. Alex gave chase. Holly kept up, adrenaline powering her alongside Alex. Terrorist and hostages alike ran for their lives. About a hundred metres ahead was an outcrop of rock thirty metres high, with a hollowed-out entrance, like a cave. A sign lay on the ground; it said: 'DANGER: MINE WORKINGS'. The entrance was blocked by a wire gate, but a big hole had been cut in it and the edges were curled inwards. Danger or not, it was shelter. Alex and Holly dived after Pirroni into the gloomy depths.

Inside, Pirroni clamped a hand around Holly's arm. She wanted to collapse and catch her breath but he held her fast and forced her to stay on her feet. 'This way.' He took her further into the cave and drew his gun. She saw it and sobbed, stumbling alongside him. Alex's blood thundered in his head. Was he about to shoot her?

Pirroni turned to face him. 'You,' he said. 'Take her other arm.'

Alex obeyed, a thousand possibilities going through his mind. Was Pirroni about to kill them? Or was he threatening Holly simply to make him behave? The terrorist led them further into the cave. Where was he taking them? Was he looking for a quiet spot to shoot them and dump their bodies? Or was he trying to find a hiding place in case they were followed into the mine by someone else looking for shelter – or looking for them?

They passed decaying pit props. No wonder the place was locked up and condemned, thought Alex. Holly sobbed quietly. She feared for her life and Alex didn't dare say anything to her. She stumbled. Alex pulled her upright and heard a skittering of rocks as though they had dislodged some stones.

Then the whole floor slid away from underneath them.

Alex was thrown onto his back. Rocks dug into his spine and he was moving fast. The floor was giving way, roaring down into a big hole that had suddenly opened up. Holly screamed, sliding past him like someone caught in an avalanche. Alex grabbed her hand and her momentum pulled him down too. They hit the bottom together. Boulders bounced around them as they crashed down to the lower level, splintering into sharp, razor-like fragments.

Alex saw a large rock. If they could hide behind it, everything would go past them. Keeping hold of

Holly, he got up, but his feet slithered on the unstable rubble. All he could do was dive for the rock and roll behind it, pulling Holly with him. It probably wasn't comfortable for her being dragged like that but it was better than leaving her. If he let go of her, he'd never find her again because he couldn't see anything. He had no idea what had happened to Pirroni.

The noise was earsplitting, crash upon crash like claps of thunder. Boulders rained down like hail. They shattered and the shrapnel cut his exposed arm like needles. The ground shook. Dust choked every breath he took and he tasted it in his mouth like cement.

Li was running hard. Behind her the orange glow of the fire ate up the trees, catching on the twigs, bark and dry leaves that littered the floor of the wood. It engulfed the termite mounds. All the animals had fled; she was the only living thing struggling to escape the flames.

She saw the entrance to the mine and dived in without hesitation. Inside, she collapsed against a rough-hewn wall, gasping for air.

At first she thought the roaring sound she could

hear was the blood in her ears. But it was coming from deep within the mine. Dust was roiling towards her like smoke. But she knew it wasn't smoke. An experienced mountaineer, she knew only too well the sound of a rockfall.

Li didn't wait to see boulders raining down. She spotted a steel cabinet and dived in, wedging the door wide open. She didn't want to be trapped if something fell in front of the door.

Tommy drove onto the road and braked. 'This is where I found you.'

'But the wreckage of the plane isn't here,' said Amber. She was mystified. For miles in either direction the road was clear.

'Maybe it blew away,' said Hex. But privately he thought Tommy was wrong too. How could he ask the Aboriginal if he was sure about the location without offending him?

Tommy seemed to read his mind. 'This tree was here,' he said, pointing. The three friends followed his gesture with their eyes. It did look like the tree they had sheltered under during the first storm, but they had passed many other trees that looked just like it too.

Tommy got out of the truck and walked round to the passenger door. 'One of you drive,' he said. 'I'll check the ground.'

Paulo shifted to the driver's seat and started the engine. 'Here's where we're going, Paulo,' said Amber. She pointed to a mark on her map.

Paulo took the truck very slowly in a big circle, covering the area identified by Amber. Then the plan was to head straight across to the centre of the circle, to the point where the seaplane was most likely to be. Tommy hung out of the open door, inspecting the orange ground for signs.

He's never going to find anything, thought Hex. There's nothing to see. The ground was so hard they could barely see the tracks of their own truck, which weighed a couple of tonnes. How would a human weighing far less leave any sort of mark? But maybe he would be able to tell if a plane had landed – or taken off again.

Tommy held up his hand. 'Stop.' Paulo braked gently, aware of his precariously balanced passenger.

They were at the edge of a wood. Tommy jumped out and squatted down on the ground. 'Animals have been this way. Two kangaroos fleeing from the fire. We must be careful.' He paused and traced his fingers lightly above the dust as though uncovering something. He added, 'Also people moving.'

Amber, Hex and Paulo jumped out of the truck. Hex and Amber squatted down on either side of Tommy. Hex peered over Tommy's shoulder. No matter how closely he looked, he could see nothing there.

'One woman, two men,' said Tommy. 'The man walks with a limp.' He stood up. 'Come. We follow them further.'

Amber glanced at Hex. She could see the same question on Hex's face as was on her own. They hadn't told Tommy about the people they were looking for. Yet Tommy knew Pirroni had a limp. Just how had he worked that out?

Paulo drove along the edge of a wood. Tommy hung out of the side looking for more tracks. But he stayed quiet for ages, finding no more sightings.

He straightened up and put a hand in the small

of his back, easing the muscles. 'The storm must have wiped the other prints away,' he said. 'I can't see them any more.' Then his face changed.

'What's the matter, Tommy?' said Amber.

Tommy sniffed the air and pulled the door closed with a slam. He pointed towards the open clearing. His voice was urgent. 'Quickly, take the truck over there and stop.'

Paulo steered around the termite mounds to where Tommy had indicated.

Tommy hopped out. 'We'll have to leave the truck here on the grass. The fire is coming.'

Amber climbed down after him. 'Wouldn't we be safer in the truck?'

Tommy shook his head. 'The truck will get too hot.'

'Like an oven, I suppose,' said Paulo. 'But why are we leaving it here?'

'If the grass catches fire it won't set fire to the truck. But if we are in the forest the truck will burn. Follow me.' He stalked off towards the wood.

Amber, Hex and Paulo followed. 'Does that make sense?' said Amber quietly to Hex.

'I suppose the forest provides more fuel – with all that leaf litter and twigs and stuff.'

Tommy reached the wood and squatted down on his haunches. When the three friends caught up with him they found him tracing a mark on a tree with his finger.

'Cut with scissors, recently,' he said. 'And here' – he placed his hand on the ground, palm down – 'here we have the footprint of a woman.'

The rockfall was over as suddenly as it had started. When the silence came Alex stayed stock-still, listening. Any moment it might start again. He held his breath. The mine stayed quiet.

He looked at Holly. Her mane of hair was clogged with red dust. He squeezed her hand and mouthed at her, 'You OK?'

Holly nodded.

Alex put his finger to his lips: Stay quiet. A little light was coming from gaps in the rock far above. The air was thick with dust. He moved and particles danced like red smoke. Around him was a chaos of smashed rocks and splintered pit props. A large piece of the floor above had collapsed, as though a car had been dropped through a house into the basement. When he looked more closely he saw why: it was concrete supported by wooden pit props – probably made to cover a natural hole in the floor. The parts that stayed standing were solid rock. Still, it looked as though nothing more was going to collapse.

He got to his feet. Holly followed. She was covered in grazes but seemed to get up OK. Nothing broken, then. Alex looked around. Where was Pirroni? There was no sign of him. Maybe he was behind some of the heaps of rubble. Maybe he was knocked out or injured. Alex's heart beat faster. Could they be free? And if they were, how would they get out?

Alex looked up at the entrance. It was a wide ledge, about five metres deep and five metres above him. It looked safe, but how would they climb up there?

Perhaps that wasn't the only way out. He looked at the debris around him. There were a few substantial boulders but beyond it was dark. If there was a way out there, it would take time to find it.

Holly leaned close to Alex and whispered, 'Where's – er – you know . . . ?'

'Hmm,' answered Alex quietly. He was keeping his emotions under iron control. It would be so easy to relax, say or do something unwise and get shot. All this time he had been co-operative and harmless, a perfectly behaved, compliant hostage. Now he boiled with excitement; they might be free. No, get a grip, he told himself. They couldn't just run away; climbing out would take time and they would be very visible. Pirroni could be watching from behind a rock and shoot them. Better make sure they were safe before they did anything else.

So where was Pirroni? He had definitely fallen with them. Alex had kept hold of Holly, which is why they had ended up together. Pirroni must have been swept in a different direction. Alex picked his way cautiously towards the biggest mound of debris.

How ridiculous, he thought. I am tiptoeing around looking for the man who has been holding me and Holly against our will. We should just turn and run for it. He picked his way around one boulder. Nothing. He stepped around the next.

Pirroni was slumped against the other side, unconscious.

Alex stared. It was like finding a vicious predator asleep in front of him. This might be a ruse. Did he dare go closer? Where was Pirroni's weapon? Look for that first.

Alex couldn't see the gun at all. He stepped closer. Yes, Pirroni was breathing. His water bottle lay smashed on the ground. The terrorist had a cut above his eye and his right arm was scraped where he had shielded himself from the pounding rocks. But there was no bleeding from the nose, mouth or ears, which would be signs of a serious injury. He had probably hit his head and been knocked out. Or was he bluffing?

Then Alex saw something. Suddenly he was sure Pirroni wouldn't be getting up and walking away. The terrorist's left hand was trapped underneath the boulder. Alex stared at it: the whole hand was under a rock the size of a demolition ball. Alex cautiously pushed it but it didn't move even a millimetre. It might as well have been cemented there.

Alex's mind raced. Should he try to get his knife? He couldn't see it, but Pirroni had been wearing it on his left side so it was probably jammed against his body. Did he dare touch the terrorist to get it?

No, this wasn't just about him. There was Holly to think of too.

He straightened up. As he made his way back to Holly, he allowed himself a smile.

21
TRAPPED

Hex, running through the wood with Amber, Paulo and Tommy, heard the crackle of the flames behind him. He glanced over his shoulder and wished he hadn't. Orange flames licked through the bush, racing along the line of trees like liquid. Whatever it touched caught in a billow of light. A wave of smoke rolled over him. He put on a spurt.

Tommy led the way. He weaved between the trees with the poise of a world-class rugby player on his way to a try. Hex fixed his eyes on him, let his legs carry him and ran for all he was worth.

Smoke caught in his throat; it was like inhaling a blanket. Hex started to cough, then the coughs possessed him like a demon. He doubled over, hacking the irritation out of his lungs. He kept putting one foot in front of the other, but once he started coughing he only wanted to cough more. Amber and Paulo flailed along beside him, hacking and spluttering, slowing like broken machines.

In front of them, Tommy had ripped off his shirt and was squatting down. He dug down into the earth with his knife and brought out a large frog. Cupping his hands around the creature's body, he squeezed gently. A stream of water came out of its mouth and hit the shirt.

Amber started to speak but her words caught in her throat and she spluttered instead.

Tommy turned the fabric until it was thoroughly soaked, then put the frog gently back on the ground. It hopped away, unharmed, back to its burrow. Tommy tore the shirt into four strips and handed them out. 'Put this over your face and breathe normally,' he said.

Hex felt a surge of heat like a blast from an oven.

He clasped the soaked fabric around his nose and mouth. Immediately the air going into his lungs cleared. He saw Amber and Paulo's expressions change as their breathing became easier; their eyes peering over the masks looked less desperate.

Hex jumped to his feet and they were all running again. He could barely see – he just kept following the tireless black figure that threaded through the bush with such certainty. A burning tree fell with a great crack in front of Tommy but he was already hurdling out of the way. He seemed to be able to predict where the flames would catch next.

Suddenly there were no longer trees around them. Tommy stopped. He squatted down. 'We rest here.'

Hex's eyes met Paulo's and Amber's, darting nervously above the masks. They were thinking the same as him. Surely they had to keep running.

'Do this,' said Tommy. He rolled into a ball, his arms holding his head tightly, like a tortoise withdrawing into its shell.

Amber, Hex and Paulo rolled up, closed their eyes and waited.

* * *

Amber felt her breathing get easier. She blinked. Her eyes stung, but they stung less. She looked around. They were on a flat patch of ground. It gleamed brilliant white in the sunlight for miles around them; it was like being in the middle of an old, cracked satellite dish.

Tommy had brought them to a clearing. The flames had come close but where they had sheltered there was nothing to burn and so they were safe. In the distance the fire crackled, but it was moving on.

Hex scratched at the ground with his fingers. It left white under his nails. He licked it cautiously. 'Salt,' he said, looking round at the others.

'Must be an ancient lake bed,' said Paulo.

Tommy stood up. 'My spirit ancestors are in this white lake.' He started walking. 'Come.'

Alex stood looking up at the ledge where the entrance to the cave was. Getting up there looked no easier close to. There was a solid, smooth rockface like a cliff wall.

Holly was beside him. 'I don't know about you,'

she said, 'but I couldn't climb up that.' They were speaking normally now and her voice echoed in the large chamber.

Alex moved closer. There were chisel marks in the rock, as though it had been hewn by tools, but they didn't offer much in the way of foot- and handholds. 'Maybe it's better further over,' he said. He ran his fingers over the rock in case the dimming light was making it look more difficult than it was. But his eyes weren't deceiving him. He let out a sigh, gazing up at the roof of the cavern in exasperation. *Think*: what could they do?

A slight figure was silhouetted against the light. 'You guys OK down there?'

Alex's heart skipped a beat. 'Li?' he shouted.

'The one and only. What's up?'

'We're stuck. We can't get out.'

Li called out, 'Where's Pirroni?'

'Immobilized. Have you got any rope up there, or something we can climb?'

'Stay there. I think I saw some.'

When she reappeared, she was swinging something nonchalantly from one hand, like a catwalk model drawing attention to an expensive accessory. She posed at the rim of the ledge.

'Li, you're a star!' exclaimed Alex.

Li looked down. 'Yep, it looks long enough. I'll find something to fix it to.' She disappeared again.

Alex saw Holly's puzzled expression and started to explain that Li was his friend, that she had been hiding in the plane, but Li returned moments later.

'Are you ready? Rope coming down.' She tossed one end down to Alex and Holly.

Alex caught the end of the rope. He steadied it and held it out to Holly. 'Can you climb a rope?'

Holly grasped the end. She had never climbed a rope in her life but Li and Alex seemed to think it was easy. 'I'll have a go.'

'I'll give you a leg up,' said Alex. He clasped her around her waist. 'On a count of three: one – two—' He launched her up.

She caught the rope and wrapped her legs around it. It was harder than she'd thought. When she moved, she swung about and it felt very unsafe.

Alex put his foot on the bottom of the rope to steady her. 'Is that better?'

Holly nodded and started to clamber up. The rope was rough, like a steel cable. Gripping it seemed to take off a layer of skin. Her thighs started to cramp from propelling herself upwards. But she made progress up the rope. She forced herself. If she couldn't, how would they get out?

'That's it,' called Alex. 'You're doing fine.' She stopped halfway up and Alex gave her some more encouragement. 'It's OK, Holly, take your time. You're doing well.'

But there was something wrong. Holly stayed where she was, clinging to the rope. Alex peered up at her. Her sides were going in and out like bellows, as though she was having trouble breathing. He caught the telltale sound of a wheeze, like when they were in the dust storm, but worse. 'Li,' he called, 'pull her up! She's got asthma!'

Li seized the rope and pulled, but Holly was heavy. Li's feet skidded on the loose stones on the floor and she started to slide towards the edge. She had to let go.

Alex called from below. 'She's stuck, Li! Quick, get her up!'

I need to ground myself, thought Li. She squatted down so that her centre of gravity was as low as possible and grasped the rope. Letting out a great roar, she pulled for all she was worth. Holly emerged over the lip of the shaft in a cloud of dust. Li caught her under her shoulders and dragged her clear, then untangled the rope, checked it was still firmly fixed to the steel cabinet and threw the free end down to Alex.

Li knelt down next to Holly. The girl was on all fours. She was trying to breathe, but every time she did, she wheezed painfully. Li peered at her face. 'Holly, listen. Do you have an inhaler?'

Holly shook her head. Li glanced at the girl's lips and hands. They were pink, not turning blue; that was a good sign.

Alex clambered out of the shaft. He dropped the rope and rushed to Holly's side.

'Quick, let's get her outside,' said Li. 'There's too much dust in here.'

They hauled the stricken girl to her feet and walked her to the entrance. Outside, the forest was smoking, the trees visible as charcoal silhouettes.

Embers still glowed but most of the flames were gone. Some smoke drifted over towards them. Holly wheezed all the harder.

'No, we're better inside,' said Alex. They turned back.

Li peered at Holly's lips. They were starting to look purplish. That meant her body was lacking oxygen. What should she do? 'Holly, speak to us,' she said urgently.

Holly managed to gasp a few words. 'I'm not usually asthmatic.' The effort was too much and she couldn't say any more.

'Must be the dust storm,' said Li. 'I've heard they can cause asthma.'

Alex looked up. 'What was that? It sounds like a truck.' He looked in the direction of the entrance.

The three froze where they were.

Hex clambered in through the hole in the wire gate. Amber and Paulo squeezed in after him.

'Well, you took your time,' said Alex.

'Are you all OK?' asked Hex. 'Where's Pirroni?'

'He's a bit stuck right now,' said Alex. 'Paulo, can you help here?'

'Her name's Holly, she's having an asthma attack and she hasn't got an inhaler,' said Li.

In seconds Paulo was by their side. 'Here, let me . . .' He slipped his arm under the shoulder that Alex was supporting. Li stepped away on the other side.

Paulo was far from certain what he was going to do. He'd read about a way to stop an asthma attack on an alternative medicine website and had no idea if it worked. But Holly's lips were turning blue. If she didn't get more oxygen she could die.

'Hi, Holly.' He gave her his most dazzling Latin smile. 'I'm Paulo. I'm going to make you feel better, and all you have to do is concentrate on what I say. If you do, you'll be fine. OK?'

Her chest heaved and her eyes looked desperate. He could see that the only thing she could think about was how she couldn't breathe.

He dug his nails into her arm. Her eyes flicked to his. She looked like a frightened deer, but at least he had her attention. 'Holly, I can help you. Will you let me help you?'

Holly made a hoarse, desperate noise. Paulo forced himself to stay calm, to take control, but she looked so distressed. Could he really cure this? 'Holly,' he repeated patiently, 'will you do as I tell you?'

She nodded.

OK. On to the next stage. 'What we're going to do is walk slowly and count. It will help you relax and breathe normally.' *Dios*, thought Paulo, this'll never work. That website must be mad. Did it say anyone had ever done this?

But Holly had no other chance. Stop doubting, Paulo thought. She has to believe I can cure her or she won't do it. And I have to believe it two hundred per cent. 'Holly,' he said firmly, 'this will work. Walk with me; keep in time with my steps. Say "One" every time you put your left foot down. Here we go.'

Paulo began to take slow steps. Holly walked beside him, making a high-pitched, whining sound. Her body was rigid with tension. Believe it will work, Paulo told himself. She will start to relax and she will be all right.

Paulo took the girl in a big circle around the cave. 'One,' he repeated every time she put her left foot down. Holly tried to count too. Instead the words came in short gasps. It sounded horrible. Stay calm, Paulo told himself. She's frightened; she has to relax. Just keep encouraging her. 'That's great,' he said. 'One; one.'

Her shoulders loosened fractionally. She was trusting him more. Her voice joined his more loudly, more surely. 'Hey,' said Paulo, 'that time you did it louder than me! Good girl.'

Li glanced at Alex. 'That looks like what you'd do with an old horse.'

'Yes, but it seems to be working,' said Alex. Holly looked calmer. She was smiling again and even managed a laugh.

Li looked around. 'We should get her away from here. The dust and smoke can't be helping.'

'We have the truck outside,' said Hex. 'I e-mailed the co-ordinates of the Aboriginal outstation to Sergeant Powell. It's a couple of hours' drive away so he'll probably be there by the time we get back.'

Tommy had come into the mine entrance to see what was going on.

Amber introduced him. 'This is Tommy – we

wouldn't have found you without his help. He would probably like to get home before dark.'

Tommy was watching Paulo. 'He has a rare healing touch,' he said.

Alex got up. 'If we're going, I'd better check on our guest. I don't want to leave him for the rats before Sergeant Powell can pick him up. Besides, he's got something of mine.' He jogged to the rope and began to climb down.

Li jumped to her feet. 'I'm coming with you.'

Hex remembered his watch. He hurried after them. 'Oi, Alex,' he called, 'you've got something of mine too.' He shinned down the rope. When he hit the bottom he saw Alex and Li staring at a boulder in the gloom.

'Is he dead?' asked Hex, approaching quietly.

Alex shook his head. He was looking down. 'No. He's gone.' His voice was clipped with barely controlled anger.

Hex looked at Li in dismay. 'I thought we had him.'

Alex squatted down on the floor. 'We did.' His voice was anguished. 'He was trapped by this rock.

He can't have got out. How could he move it from down on the floor?'

He squatted down to look more closely at the dusty ground. There had to be an explanation. It just wasn't possible . . .

Li stepped towards him. 'Alex, he's gone. No-one expected you to catch him—' Something caught her eye and she leaped back with a strangled scream. 'What's that?'

'Oh my God,' said Hex. 'Alex, it's down by your boot.'

Alex looked at his right boot. He recoiled.

Li felt sick. 'It's his hand.'

Where the rock had trapped Pirroni's hand, they could see a bloody stump. A pool of red oozed from it.

Alex steadied himself against the boulder. It was a moment before he could speak. When he did, his voice was hoarse. 'He freed himself,' he said slowly, 'by sawing off his own hand.'

22
Blood in the Sand

Alex waited for the waves of nausea to pass. Li kept her hand over her mouth for several minutes.

'He must have used my knife,' said Alex eventually.

Hex swallowed and looked around the shadowy cavern. 'Where can he have gone?'

'He must still be here somewhere,' said Li. She knelt down gingerly. 'Where's his gun?' She tried not to look at the gruesome thing poking out from under the rock.

'I had a look for that,' said Alex. 'He's probably

still got it.' He stood up again and kicked the rock. 'Damn!'

Hex manoeuvred around the two of them and squatted on the ground. 'He must have left a trail. Let's get Tommy.'

'OK, but you stay up there with the others. Tell them to get in the truck and leave the engine running. We don't want him sneaking up and taking more hostages.'

Tommy examined the signs left by Pirroni. 'The man who limps. He was bleeding.'

Li asked, 'Did he come back this way and up the rope?'

Tommy shook his head. 'No.' He pointed into the darkness. 'He went this way.' The bushman got up and began to follow the trail.

Alex put a hand on his shoulder. 'No, Tommy,' he said. 'He's got a gun. It's too dangerous. You've done enough for us already.'

Paulo was waiting in the truck with Hex, Amber and Holly.

Li and Tommy came out of the mine entrance. Alex appeared last. He strode up to Paulo. 'It's not safe here. Pirroni could be anywhere and he might come back. Take them back to Tommy's people and bring Sergeant Powell out here.'

Paulo looked at him suspiciously. 'Why are you telling me this now? You could tell me when we're on our way.'

'I'm not coming,' said Alex. 'I'm going to stay here so we don't lose Pirroni again.'

Hex was horrified. 'You can't, Alex . . .' He climbed out of the truck. Amber followed.

Alex shook his head vehemently. 'I shouldn't have let him go. We have a blood trail; I can track him with that and lead Sergeant Powell to him.'

'I'm staying too,' Li insisted

Hex was beside her. 'And me.'

By now Paulo was out of the truck too. 'We're all coming.'

Holly got out slowly and watched them from a distance. She had the feeling she shouldn't interrupt.

Alex gathered his friends together and spoke in a low voice. It would be better if Holly didn't hear.

'Paulo, you need to look after Holly. If she gets another attack you're the only one who knows what to do.'

Then he turned to Li. 'Li, you go. You've been out in the bush as long as I have. You need the rest.'

'You don't look so good yourself,' she countered.

Amber spoke before Alex could get to her. 'I'm coming. You need me to navigate. The compasses are useless here and you'll just go round in circles.'

Alex looked at Hex. 'Hex, you don't have to stay.'

'No,' said Hex. 'I'm not leaving you again.' He unclipped his palmtop in its carrying case from his waistband and gave it to Li. 'Use this to contact Sergeant Powell when you get to the outstation. They haven't got modems there and this is the only way to e-mail anyone.'

Li took it from him reverently. 'You're trusting me with your precious palmtop?'

'Well aren't you the lucky one,' said Amber. 'I thought it was surgically attached to him.'

Hex wanted to snatch it straight back. Instead he began to gabble instructions. 'It's out of batteries but it's set for the power supply at the outstation so all you have to do is plug it in. Don't change anything. You'll find all the settings as they should be . . . the power lead is in there . . . Don't change—'

Li held up a hand. 'I'll wipe out your website favourites and replace them with fluffy pink girly ones. Come on, Paulo.'

'Don't touch anything—' Li heard the anguished wail behind her.

Tommy was in the driving seat, waiting.

Holly hadn't heard what Alex had said but she understood that he wasn't coming. She came forward and put a hand on his arm. 'You're staying here? Why? We're free at last.'

Alex looked at her. Should he explain? No, he couldn't. 'Go with Paulo. He'll get you to safety. He's a good friend.'

She nodded slowly, then turned on her heel.

Alex, Hex and Amber watched them drive away. The sun was setting. All the dust and smoke in the atmosphere made it spectacular. The clouds turned vivid red like liquid lava sprayed across the deepening blue sky. The skeletons of the burned trees showed in silhouette against the last rays of the day.

Holly looked back at the mine. She thought she knew Alex. But why was he deliberately staying where he was, in danger? And who were these friends of his, who seemed as extraordinarily brave as he was? How did they come out of nowhere like that? She looked at the set faces of Paulo and Li and realized that her questions would have to wait.

Alex strode back into the mine. He headed straight for the rope, climbed down and went to the trail of Pirroni's blood. A rat was nibbling at the hand. It scurried away as he approached.

Amber and Hex followed him. 'Alex, what are you doing?'

Amber registered out of the corner of her eye the thing that lay under the rock. 'Oh my God,' she groaned. 'Is that . . .' She felt her stomach turn over.

Alex knelt on his hands and knees. Where was the trail of blood that Tommy had picked out? Were those spots of blood? The ground was red so it was hard to tell. He stood up. Tommy had said they went further into the mine. Suddenly he felt unsteady. He put out his hand and leaned on the boulder.

'Alex, we can't follow him now.' Hex's voice was firm. 'It's nearly dark outside – there's no light at all in here. Anyway, we don't know where that goes.'

'And you can barely stand up,' added Amber. 'You need to rest.'

Alex squinted at the ground. Tommy had seen the blood. Surely he could too. There was no time to lose. 'You go and rest,' said Alex savagely. 'I have to find him.'

Amber looked helplessly at Hex. She took a small piece of root out of her pocket and proffered it to him. 'Suck this and swallow the fluid.'

Alex took his hand off the rock, intending to take the root, but swayed again. 'What is it?' he said suspiciously.

Amber leaned over and pinched him on the arm. Alex looked shocked. She pinched him again and watched the skin. Just as she thought – instead of springing back quickly, it remained in a peak and subsided slowly. 'You're dehydrated,' she said.

'That's why you're unco-ordinated.' She held out the root again.

Alex looked at his arm where Amber had pinched him. Slowly, he took the root from her. 'What is it?'

Hex was leaning against the wall looking at him. 'Water tree root. Tommy showed us how to find them. That's how we've been getting water.'

With a dubious expression on his face, Alex put the root to his lips and sucked. He was expecting it to taste nasty but it was refreshing and succulent.

'Another,' said Amber. 'That's an order, not a question.'

Alex took more of the roots and sucked them. He started to look steadier. 'Actually, guys,' he said, 'I feel a bit better.'

'Be thankful she's not making you kiss a frog,' said Hex.

They made their camp for the night in the entrance chamber of the mine, well away from the chasm in the floor. Hex built a small fire in a rusting oil drum so that they would have warmth and light. Amber left them to go looking for food.

Hex went outside once the fire was stable. Alex was digging a hole at the edge of the wood where the ashy ground was soft. He had found a plastic container and some polythene sheeting in the mine. He placed the container in the bottom of the hole and covered it with a sheet of plastic in the shape of a cone.

Alex looked up at Hex. 'I'm making a solar still. It'll give us plenty of water by morning. Of course, it will need to be boiled first but—'

'Forgive me for being thick,' said Hex, 'but – er – the sun has gone down and it's not coming back until morning.'

'The earth's still warm from the fire,' replied Alex. 'Overnight the soil will release quite a lot of condensation.' He stood up. 'Help me make another here.'

They finished the second still and went back into the mine. Amber strode in. 'Hey, guys, I caught us dinner.' She had taken off her scarf and was using it to cradle something.

At the thought of food, Alex's eyes grew enormous. He hadn't realized how hungry he was. 'Great! I'm starving.'

Amber put the bundle down carefully. 'Have we got anything to cook on? A skewer or something?' She unzipped her medical pouch and took her evening dose of insulin.

'I'm afraid my knife is temporarily unavailable,' said Alex darkly. But he couldn't help feeling brighter. If skewers were needed, what had Amber caught? Were they having kangaroo steaks roasted over the fire?

'Hex,' said Amber, 'have you got something in that tool kit we can use?'

'Under no circumstances are you using my tools to spit-roast outback wildlife,' said Hex emphatically. Then he pulled himself up. He suddenly knew what Amber had wrapped in her scarf.

'I don't know how long you cook these for,' she said, and folded back the corners. Inside were six live witchetty grubs. 'Tommy showed me how to find them.'

Hex struggled to hide his disgust. They were white with a pointed black head that moved around slowly, like a giant maggot blindly looking for something. But then he glanced across at Alex, whose expression was quite the most entertaining thing he had seen for days – a mixture of revulsion and deep disappointment. He looked like a little kid who'd been told Christmas had been cancelled. 'Oh yum, witchetty grubs,' said Hex with feigned enthusiasm. 'Amber, you really know the way to a man's heart.'

'You cannot be serious,' exclaimed Alex. He looked from Hex to Amber and back again.

Hex unfolded his tool kit and selected a couple of screwdrivers. They were old and he'd intended to replace them anyway.

Amber caught his eye and smirked. She took a screwdriver and bashed the grubs with the blunt end to kill them, then threaded them on like kebabs. Laying them across the flames, she told them, 'Tommy said ten of these will keep a man going for an entire day.'

There was a loud bang. The truck came to a screeching stop. Li had dozed off against Paulo's shoulder but was suddenly wide awake. Paulo shifted away from her and darted out of the cab.

'What happened?' asked Li.

Holly was next to her, also looking around in a panic. 'I don't know. I think we hit something. I was asleep.'

'What's that noise?' said Li. There was a loud hissing. It was coming from the front of the truck. She cupped her hands and peered through the windscreen. In the light of the headlamps, she saw Tommy heft up the body of a kangaroo. It was large and lifting it took all his strength. He staggered round to the back of the truck and tipped it onto the flat bed. The truck bounced on its axles.

Li climbed out. Paulo was at the front of the truck. When he saw Li he shook his head. 'It's the radiator,' he said. 'I'd better look under the bonnet. Stand back.' He walked round to the driver's side and pulled the bonnet release. As the metal lifted, a geyser of steam poured out with an angry hiss. Paulo dodged out of the way. '*Mal suerte*,' he muttered.

'That doesn't sound good,' said Li. She could just about see Paulo's grave expression in the headlights.

'It is not,' said Paulo. 'Coolant is leaking, fast.'

Tommy came round to the front. By now Holly had climbed out too.

'The truck is undriveable,' said Paulo.

'So I suppose we're stuck here for the night?' Holly sounded resigned.

'We can't wait here,' said Li. 'We have to get a message to Sergeant Powell. We'll have to walk. Tommy, can you navigate by the stars?'

It was Paulo who replied. 'How do you think he got us here in the first place?'

'Sorry,' mumbled Li. 'Tired and not thinking.'

Paulo hadn't realized how exhausted Li was. Normally she'd have bitten his head off for a remark like that, not meekly accepted it.

Tommy turned off the headlights. In the darkness Li just wanted to sleep there and then. She stood for a moment with her eyes closed.

Paulo put a hand on her shoulder. 'Are you all right?'

Li nodded.

'Have you got Hex's palmtop?'

Li panicked. She had forgotten about that. But when she patted her belt it was still firmly attached. She breathed a sigh of relief. 'If I lost that I might as well join the French Foreign Legion.'

Paulo looked at Holly. She looked exhausted too. 'Holly, we can stay here if you want while Li and Tommy get help. We'll be all right in the truck.'

'Out here in the dark? No thanks, mate,' retorted Holly. 'No offence, but I've had enough of the outback. I'm coming with you.'

They started walking. Paulo kept a close eye on Holly. She kept stumbling. In spite of her feisty words she was very, very tired. He hoped fervently that the journey wouldn't be very long.

Hex used Amber's scarf to clean his screwdrivers. Amber treated Alex's cuts with the antiseptic Li had brought from the plane.

Alex flinched. 'I reckon Pirroni will be holed up somewhere, probably near here.'

'He might have died,' said Amber. 'We might just find a body.' She dabbed at another cut. The antiseptic cleaned off the dust ingrained in Alex's face so that pale skin showed through in patches. It looked rather peculiar. 'Boy,' she smirked, 'you really need to cleanse, tone and moisturize.'

Alex could only think of the task ahead. 'Then we

go out and find his body. But whatever happens, we find him.' He winced as Amber tackled a deep gash.

Hex threw some more dried sticks on the fire. 'How do you reckon we'll catch him, though, Alex? He's still got his gun.'

Alex had thought about this. 'We don't have to. I reckon that by tomorrow, if he's still alive, he'll be dehydrated. He'll be making bad decisions. So we don't have to capture him or even approach him, just keep him moving. We maintain the pressure on him until he can't go any further.'

'Like hunting a fox to exhaustion,' said Hex.

'Exactly,' said Alex emphatically, adding, without a trace of humour, 'And then I'll get my knife back.'

Paulo had absolute faith in Tommy's navigation, but the walk seemed to go on and on. Without the truck's headlights the outback night was very dark – there was a little ambient light from the stars, and the moon was showing its first quarter. They could just about make out each other's outlines, but little else. As they walked they held onto each other, picking their way carefully like climbers on a tricky rock face.

Holly was leaning on him heavily. She was ready to drop. Li stumbled. In the pitch blackness it was hard to negotiate the rough ground.

Suddenly Tommy said, 'Stop. Listen.' The party froze. 'Dingo,' he said, and moved off, pulling Paulo by his arm. Paulo hadn't been aware of anything. How did Tommy hear so much?

Paulo was preoccupied with Holly's breathing. He kept listening for the telltale signs of another asthma attack. They could be brought on by stress, and the girl had suffered more in the past few days than any normal teenager could be expected to cope with. If it happened again, his walking cure might not be enough – recurrences were often more severe.

Tommy stopped. 'Listen.' They stood still.

This time Paulo heard it; he thought he was hallucinating that he was back on his ranch. 'A horse,' he said softly. He gently disengaged his hand from Holly's and stepped forwards.

There was a gentle snort, the traditional equine greeting. Paulo put his hand out. Warm breath caressed his fingers. He let the horse sniff him and then gently put his other hand out and touched a solid neck. The horse tensed and pulled away. They heard the beat of its hooves as it trotted off a short way and then stopped.

Paulo, unperturbed, approached again. This time the horse let him stroke it for longer. He could feel the tension in its muscles. Paulo talked to it and slowly it began to relax.

Li felt a large presence near her. Gentle blasts of warm air investigated her fingers. A huge head was silhouetted against the moon. 'Paulo,' she whispered, 'there's another one. What do I do to be friends with it?'

'Just let it touch you, and gently stroke it. They communicate by touch.'

'Are they wild?' whispered Holly.

'No,' said Paulo. He ran his fingers over the horse's warm body, feeling its shoulders, back and quarters. 'They are muscled to carry riders.'

'Well deduced, Dr Dolittle. Nothing to do with that bridle on its head,' said Li. She managed to load a lot of scorn into a whisper.

'It's a headcollar, not a bridle,' said Paulo. He

kept stroking the horse, reassuring it that he could be trusted. 'Li, will that horse let you get on?'

Li scowled at him. 'Er, how do I do that exactly?'

'Just grasp the mane and swing yourself up. Like this.' In a moment Paulo's silhouette was looking down at the rest of the party. He patted the horse.

Li launched herself up. She found herself sitting on the horse's back. 'Now what?'

'Talk to it, stroke it. It's not a machine.' Paulo dismounted. 'Holly, I will help you up.'

'I can't ride,' said Holly.

'You don't have to,' said Paulo. 'Just hold onto the mane and relax. I will stay at its head. It will be a lot less tiring for you than walking.' He hoisted her onto the horse.

'Paulo,' said Li, 'something tells me you've got a plan.'

'These horses are well looked after. We must be close to a ranch or farm. Horses always know their way home, so if we just let them take us, we will come to a place where we can get help. Look – he's off now.' The horse beside him started striding along. He allowed it to choose the direction and followed its lead.

Li's horse walked quietly behind Paulo's. Li gave herself up to the regular swing of the movement. It was a relief to be transported again. 'Paulo,' she said, 'just one thing. If these horses know their way home, how come they're out here?'

It was Tommy, walking beside her, who answered. 'They broke away during the fire. They have the smell of smoke in their hair.'

Amber was going to take first watch while Hex and Alex lay down to rest. She got to her feet and walked slowly around the cave. Something caught her eye in the flickering firelight and she stopped for a better look.

Alex was fast asleep, but Hex was still awake. He saw Amber looking at the cave wall. 'What is it?' he whispered.

'Tommy's left us a drawing.'

Hex got up and padded over. Amber was looking at a crude outline in white on the brown of the cave wall. It showed a white disc surrounded by flames. Elongated stick figures stood in the centre.

'It's his spirit ancestor,' she said. 'To protect us.'

23
The Hunt

The horses clattered into a concrete yard, their hooves echoing around the buildings. Lights came on, triggered by the movement. They revealed a quadrangle of farm buildings, burnt out and still smouldering.

'Looks like this is the place,' said Paulo. 'What a mess.'

Li and Holly slid quietly off the horses. 'Someone's noticed us arrive,' said Li.

A figure emerged from the house and ran towards them. A female voice called out, 'Goldie? Tess? Oh my God!'

'They're here and they're safe,' replied Paulo.

'How did you find them?' The horses greeted her with nuzzles and whickers.

'Our truck broke down and we found them loose in the outback,' said Paulo.

A man ran out of the house to join them. 'Darling, look,' said the woman. She examined one of the horses, running her hands over its legs, checking for injuries. 'Not even a scratch on them.'

The man, who Paulo assumed must be her husband, checked the other horse. 'I can't tell you how much this means to us,' he said. He looked up from examining the horse's front hoof. 'We put the horses in the barn when the fires started but a spark must have been blown into the hay. We thought we'd lost them.' He put the foot down and went to the rear one. 'How did you know they came from here?'

Paulo grinned. 'They told me. Could I ask a favour?'

'Anything,' said the man.

'Could we use your phone?'

* * *

Hex wiped his screwdrivers clean again after a breakfast of more roasted witchetty grubs. Alex poured the last of the water collected from the solar stills into bottles. The stills had worked well. Amber put the fire out with sand and spread out the embers thinly, mixing them with loose sand so that they would not be a danger.

Alex handed the water bottles around. 'OK,' he said. 'Remember: we find our man, follow him and leave a trail so that Paulo and Sergeant Powell can pick him up. Pirroni is dehydrated, tired, hungry, in pain and losing blood.'

'We, on the other hand,' said Hex with a poker-straight face, 'have had plenty of grub.'

Amber let out a yowl of laughter and thumped Hex on the back. Even Alex had to smile.

'Right,' said Amber, shouldering Li's medical kit. 'Let's go to work.'

They climbed down the rope.

'It's a bit lighter now,' said Amber, looking around when they got to the bottom. High up in the roof of the mine were small holes, probably for ventilation, but they also let the light in.

'Hopefully we'll be able to see more than when we were down here with Tommy,' said Alex.

Hex and Amber followed him to the rock where Pirroni had been trapped. Alex knelt down and looked closely. 'Got you,' he said. The blood showed as dark spots against the red earth.

'Hey, this place is like one of those tombs where the sun comes in at different angles depending on what time of day it is,' said Amber. 'Look.'

'A tunnel. Well, that makes life easier.' Hex looked at Alex. 'Is that where the trail goes?'

Alex's mouth worked into a smile. 'It certainly does.' He straightened up and stepped into the mouth of the tunnel. 'We can't be complacent, though. It may look straightforward but there might be forks or shafts – and we haven't got a torch so we won't be able to see them. Amber, you check the left-hand side, Hex, you check the right. Leave marks so we can find our way back, but not so they cover Pirroni's trail.'

'How do you know he's gone on through the tunnel?' said Amber.

'The only way we'll know that is if we find his

blood at the other end. Wherever that is. Come on.'

Alex could hardly believe it when the tunnel emerged into the open and the heat hit him like a sauna. 'Well, here we are,' he said. 'The question is, are we still on the trail?'

Hex knelt and searched the red sand. 'Yes, we are. And this looks like one of his prints.'

'How do you know?' said Amber.

'The print of the lame foot is blurred, as though it's skidding along the ground. The other carries more pressure on the ball of the foot. Tommy showed it to me.'

'Aren't you a diligent student,' said Amber. Although her tone was jokey, she was impressed: Hex had taken the opportunity to extend his skills. And locals, as they had been taught in their training, could often be invaluable in giving information about an area.

'Just move your foot a moment,' said Hex.

'Why?' said Amber, lifting her boot.

Hex traced his finger around the footprint she had

left. 'Tommy said I can tell your weight from it—Ow!' Amber had put her foot down on his finger.

'The blood is less visible out here,' said Alex. 'He must have paused to bind the wound so that it wouldn't leave so much of a trail.'

'Before we go haring off,' said Amber, 'remember he laid a false trail in the plane. He might have done it again.'

'Good thinking,' said Alex. 'Let's check.'

They walked slowly around the entrance to the tunnel. Hex squatted down in the sand to get a closer look at some marks, but they weren't footprints. He continued searching.

'Hex, is this him?' said Alex.

Hex tiptoed over, careful not to create more prints to confuse matters. 'Yes – looks like it.'

'Right,' said Alex. 'We have two sets of prints, each heading in a different direction. Which one do we take?'

'Well, he's probably going south, like he was before,' said Amber.

Alex lined his watch up on the sun to get a direction reading. 'Neither of these tracks is going south.'

Amber frowned. 'Are you sure?' she said. She checked with her watch too. 'Hmm, you're right.'

'Wait a minute,' said Hex. 'Alex, is he using a compass?'

'There's one in the survival kit he took from me.'

'Well, if he's using that, the iron in the rocks will distort the reading so he might think he's going south when . . .'

'What we need is another compass so that we know what he thinks is south,' sighed Alex.

'Wait a mo,' said Amber. She dug into the medical kit and brought out a needle and a piece of suture thread. She stroked the needle on her shirt to magnetize it and tied the thread around the middle, then held the thread so that the needle dangled from it horizontally. 'Makeshift compass,' she said with a smile. The magnetized needle swung gently until it settled in one position. 'I think you'll find that Pirroni thinks south is . . . thataway.'

'That's this track here,' said Hex.

'Got him.' Alex's voice was dark with resolve. They had discovered a small chink in the armour of this formidable man.

The tracks crested a hill. Down below, in a shallow valley, was a clump of trees and beyond it a sea of mud.

'Could be a water hole,' said Amber. She ran down the hill.

'It *was* a water hole, you mean,' said Alex. 'Quite recently too, by the look of it.' The wet mud was beginning to dry as it baked in the fierce sun.

'We should find some nice prints in that mud,' said Hex as he followed.

'Alex,' called Amber. She was in the trees on the far side. 'There's something here. I think it's the water hole's last customer.' They heard her moving further into the undergrowth. Then she screamed.

Hex reached her first. He spluttered when he saw what she was looking at. 'Ugh, that is really gross.'

It was the huge bulk of a dead camel. The abdomen was split open in a bloody line and the intestines spilled out. Flies coated the slippery grey entrails in a thick crawling veil. The smell was fetid and overpowering.

There were also flies covering a blackish object

the size of a rugby ball that lay discarded a short distance from the main incision.

'What's that?' said Amber. Her hand was over her mouth.

Alex prodded it with his boot. A cloud of flies rose up, buzzing angrily, giving him a glimpse of a fleshy white object streaked with blood. Next to it was a clump of fibrous stuff twisted like a large, fat rope.

'That's the stomach, isn't it?' said Amber through her fingers. 'What's he done?'

Alex moved away. 'He's opened it, wrung out the camel's breakfast like a dishcloth and drunk the water. Goodness knows how he killed it one-handed. It must have been sick or old and weak.'

Hex was standing near the head. Blood oozed from a wound in the animal's jugular, studded with flies. The eye sockets were a seething mass of insects. Hex tilted the camel's head with his boot just long enough to get a good look, then turned away quickly, wincing. 'He's had the eyes. There's water in them too.'

Amber moved to the animal's head, trying not to look at the fly-filled eye sockets. She put her hand at the base of the camel's ears. When she had horses, this was how she measured their core temperature. 'It's still warm. It hasn't been dead long. He's not far off.'

Alex dragged his foot through the mud to draw a large arrow. When he next spoke his voice was low and harsh. 'We've been too careless. We've forgotten that he is armed and very dangerous. From now on we proceed with the utmost caution and in silence.'

24
Closer

Pirroni walked on. He kept his pace steady. If he conserved energy he had a chance of surviving. He only had to find a truck or car, or another plane and then he could be on his way. He cradled the stump where his left hand had been, making a makeshift sling out of his good arm. The pain hit him in waves, but he was used to the idea that pain was the way to freedom.

He had feigned unconsciousness when the kid came looking for him. He could have shot him but it was better to get away. Better to save a bullet. The kid would have plenty to do trying to get himself and the girl out anyway. He'd had more important things to worry about. As long as they knew where he was he was vulnerable, so he had unthreaded his belt, made a tourniquet and set to work with Alex's knife. Every cut was a step to freedom. A crushed hand was probably no use to him anyway.

All the time he was cutting he listened. If anyone came back and found what he was doing, he would shoot.

When it was done he had ripped the sleeve off his shirt and tied it to the stump to staunch the flow of blood. He could see there was a tunnel so he had headed along it to find a place to lie low. When the kid came back later and found the hand, he had been just metres away in the dark. It was lucky coming across the camel like that; it had been lying down, so perhaps it had been on its last legs anyway. That water had saved his life.

The stump was bleeding again. He knew it would from time to time; the tourniquet was imperfect. He adjusted it, pulling the free end with his teeth.

He heard a scream ring through the bush. It sounded human. He stopped. Had he made the noise or had it come from somewhere else? He heard nothing further. He checked his compass and made sure that Alex's sheathed knife was still in the waistband of his jeans. Then he corrected his course and resumed his journey.

When Hex examined the distinctive tracks they were heavier. Pirroni must have been walking more slowly. He nodded to Alex and Amber.

They were at the edge of a wood. Ravaged by the fires, the trees were reduced to desolate stalks of charcoal, their trunks and major branches all that remained. There was a splash of blood on the red earth.

'Here he is,' said Hex. Alex nodded grimly.

They heard something moving ahead. Alex signalled 'Silence' to the others. Treading very carefully, they stepped into the wood.

The ashy surface absorbed the sound of their footfalls. All the twigs and dead leaves had been consumed by the fires, so they were able to move swiftly and quietly. Still they walked with great care, never taking their safety for granted. The trail was less obvious. The blood was harder to see on the dark floor and the prints were less clear. Did Pirroni know he was being followed?

Alex saw him first – a pale blue shirt that showed up clearly against the black and red landscape. Alex realized that if Pirroni was so visible, they must be too. He gave the signal to get down. Amber and Hex dropped silently to the ground and looked at him, awaiting the next instruction.

He reached down to his boots, still caked with clumps of red mud from the water hole. He smeared the mud across his face, the back of his neck, behind his ears. Hex and Amber understood and began to camouflage each other. When they had done their skin they put it on their clothes. Then they took up handfuls of the ashy earth and rubbed it through their hair, caking it on top of the mud.

Alex rolled cautiously into a crouching position. Pirroni's pale blue shirt was visible some distance ahead.

* * *

Pirroni continued his slow, steady walk. Flies buzzed around his stump, looking for the liquid that seeped through the makeshift bandage. They buzzed around his eyes, nose and mouth. He didn't waste energy swatting them away; there were more important things to worry about.

He didn't know how far he would have to walk, but that didn't matter. He just walked. When he was flying over the area he had seen there were farms and Aboriginal settlements. He would come to one soon. Or if he found a road he could flag down a vehicle. In that case, his wound would be a very useful way of attracting help.

He heard a sound behind him. Without thinking he had turned and fired. Then he listened for the sound of a body falling; that was also automatic. There was only the screech of birds. He stood stock-still until the sounds subsided. Perhaps it had just been a branch falling. He reminded himself that a monotonous landscape was the most tricky of all to stay alive in. It allowed your mind to wander and played tricks with it.

* * *

When Pirroni fired, Alex and the others threw themselves to the ground. Alex kept absolutely still. The terrorist stood like a statue, waiting to see if there was any further noise of someone following. Amber and Hex watched Alex for the next signal to go on. Alex stayed where he was. He wouldn't move until Pirroni did. Wounded or not, the terrorist was still a crack shot and he had bullets in his gun.

Pirroni moved his hand to his tourniquet, gripped one end of the belt in his teeth and yanked it. Alex wondered whether the bleeding was becoming worse.

Then Pirroni set off again.

Alex signalled to Hex and Amber. They got noiselessly to their feet and followed.

Pirroni walked doggedly. He tripped, put his left arm out to stop himself falling and cracked his stump on a tree. He paused and composed himself. Alex froze, his mind reeling. What sort of pain was the man coping with? His spirit of determination was unbelievable.

Was it Alex's imagination or did he see bright-red blood spurting from the wound? Pirroni adjusted the tourniquet again. He resumed walking.

For the three followers, it was a trial of nerves. Amber and Hex had to put their faith in Alex. Their plan was to trail Pirroni, however long it took. They had to be patient, keep their concentration, stay vigilant and cautious. If anyone's mind wandered the consequences could be serious. Everyone had a part to play. And they had to believe that the plan would work.

But Alex's job was harder. He had to keep his faith in himself. The others were with him because he had decided to do this. How long should they continue to follow a dangerous man with a gun? Pirroni's movements looked as if they were beginning to falter, but Alex couldn't be sure. If he was slowing down, should they take the advantage and do something while they had the chance?

No, appearances could be deceptive. Heroics were both dangerous and unnecessary. All they had to do was keep Pirroni in sight, leaving signs for Sergeant Powell and his men.

But what if Sergeant Powell didn't come? What if Paulo and Li hadn't managed to get the message to them?

They came to a clearing with termite mounds. As Amber carved an arrow into the ground, Hex spotted something down there. He knelt down to check; it was a set of human tracks. The termite mounds had acted as a firebreak and so the ground had not been scoured clean by the blaze like other areas of the wood. Hex glanced at Alex and pointed at them.

Alex dropped to his haunches to inspect them more closely.

Pirroni checked his compass again. His hand went to his water bottle. Then he remembered it had been smashed in the rockfall. Was that yesterday or this morning? He tugged on his tourniquet – now an automatic reaction. He stared at the stump. Did that happen yesterday or the day before?

He heard a sound. His right hand let go of the tourniquet, drew his gun and fired in one split second. A wallaby hit the ground and lay there. A waste of a bullet; it was too small to be worth gutting for water. Its paws continued to make running motions, as though it was dreaming.

Pirroni checked his compass again and walked on.

Alex found a vivid splash of blood on the termite mound. There were human tracks but it was confusing – two sets of Pirroni's and two sets of other tracks too.

Hex looked at them closely, then straightened up. He pointed at Alex and then at the sole of his boot.

Of course. They were Alex's own tracks. He and Holly had come this way with Pirroni. The terrorist was walking round in big circles. He was relying on the compass and it was leading him astray; clearly exhaustion and pain were also taking their toll. Another tiny chink in the man's armour.

Alex got up and motioned the others on. He heard a beating in the air and a shadow slid along the ground. A helicopter was flying overhead. It was quite high up, but it could be coming to drop off Sergeant Powell and his patrol. Alex dragged his foot along the ground to leave a mark.

Amber spotted another mark on the ground, like a large skid mark. She pointed it out silently to

Alex, who nodded. It was his own mark, left the first time round. Optimism surged inside him. This was going to work.

Ahead, Pirroni stopped. Alex, Amber and Hex froze. With their camouflage the wood was thick enough to shield them if they remained entirely still.

The helicopter circled round again, lower. Air currents disturbed some of the burned leaf litter as it passed above them. It was looking for something.

Amber saw a curiously shaped twig tumbling towards her in the downdraught of the helicopter. She caught it and held it out to Alex on the palm of her hand.

Alex stared at it. It was charred, and shaped like a letter N. He signalled to Amber and Hex to stay behind. The twig in his hand was the marker he had left on Pirroni's booby trap. Urgently, he gave another hand signal to his friends: *Don't move, stay totally still.* Amber and Hex froze, their training coming into effect instantly at Alex's signal.

At that moment there was a sudden bang like a gunshot. The three friends threw themselves down. The ground heaved into the sky. Red dust, black ashes and other detritus came raining down. Then there was silence.

Very carefully, Alex looked up.

Hex lifted his head. He hissed. 'What—?' and stopped, his eyes fixed ahead.

'Oh my God,' said Amber softly.

Pirroni was on the ground, face down. Both legs had disappeared in a mess of blood and bone. They twitched, sending out bright spurts. His mouth made a gurgling sound and blew red bubbles. There was no faking this time. He had stepped onto his own booby trap. His battered body let out a sound like a sigh and then was still.

Alex stood up and approached him. No expression crossed his face as he bent down and drew his knife with its sheath from Pirroni's waistband.

Then he turned his back on the body.

'We've finished?' said Amber, looking up at him.

Alex nodded and sat down beside her.

'Helicopters will be here soon,' said Hex.

25
Uluru

A week later, Alex sat beside his father in the shadow of Ayers Rock, the vast monolith that formed the most famous landmark of the outback. A 4x4 stood next to them, hired in Alice Springs for the trip.

Ayers Rock was a majestic sight – hundreds of metres tall and several kilometres long, stranded in the middle of empty desert. The sun was going down and the orange rock, made of arkosic sandstone, was turning crimson. Alex decided he preferred the Aboriginal name, Uluru. It conjured up all the sacred sites that lay nearby, where the spirits of ancestral beings were seen in rock formations, forests and even the red sand. Alex could relate to that. A week after his ordeal had finished, he was constantly reminded of it in the shape of a tree or the marks in a sandhill.

Alex, Hex and Amber had been found easily by the SAS squad. Paulo and Li had contacted Sergeant Powell from the farm and, with the help of Tommy, identified the position of the mine workings. When the soldiers had arrived there, they had simply followed the trail left by Amber, Hex and Alex and found the little group waiting, the ravaged body of the terrorist lying nearby.

For two days Alpha Force had stayed in their hotel, resting, recuperating and getting their strength back after their debriefing. Then, their work over, Amber and Hex had set off to go diving in the Great Barrier Reef, while Paulo had taken Li back to his ranch to continue her riding lessons. The professionals still had some tidying up to do, however; Interpol had gone to US Penitentiary Beaumont to see the man who was serving several life sentences under Pirroni's name. They had needed to show him photographs of Pirroni's remains before he had finally confessed that the two had swapped places after Pirroni had arranged for his family to be taken hostage. Alex hoped that the man and his family would now be reunited.

The TV company had enjoyed massive publicity as a result of the siege, and recruited six more celebrity contestants to live in the camp and play the games. The original six went back to their families and disappeared from the public eye. Alex was told that Holly had been whisked away to an exclusive health farm before soldiers, police counsellors and the press could get to her. He had thought that was the last he would hear of her, but the day they were leaving the hotel a postcard had arrived.

He got it out again now. It was a promotional card for a tour by McKenzie Ferrian, Holly's father. On the back, Holly had written: 'Dad's next album's out soon: look for the song by me.'

For himself, after a few days of twenty-first-century comforts Alex had been itching to be where he felt most at home: in the middle of nowhere with a survival kit and a tent. When his dad had turned up on leave and suggested seeing the sights of Australia, it couldn't have been more perfect.

Now, Alex looked at his father's face. He recognized his own grey eyes and blond hair, the expression inscrutable. Not for the first time on that trip, Alex wondered if his dad had just come from a mission. Quite often after he returned on leave, he would be a very quiet presence in the house, as if he was surfacing from an ocean of experiences he could never speak of. Alex had learned to respect that silence.

Uluru turned pink, red and purple. Finally the light faded, to leave only the stars in the clear desert night.

Alex's dad spoke. 'I've seen worse sunsets.'

'You've probably seen a lot more than me, old man,' Alex replied.

'Ah, the youth of today. No respect. What would the army have done with you?'

Alex smiled grimly. 'Yeah. Right.'

Alex's father was silent for a moment, as though choosing his next words very carefully. 'There are many people who don't fit in with the regular army. But the army isn't everything. Some of the problems in the world today need quite different solutions.'

He paused to see how his words were being received. Alex was silent, his mouth a tight line.

His dad carried on. 'Soldiering has changed. Wars are not just about armies any more. They're about small battles that ordinary people don't even know about. We need different kinds of soldiers to fight those battles. There are people on the lookout for those kinds of soldiers, Alex. They're never wasted.'

Alex was very still. From time to time, he blinked – his only movement.

His father had one last thing to say: 'What you have to do now is keep going, keep studying, keep learning. I know you've wanted this for a long time, and I know how disappointed you are.' He paused. 'But believe me, it's not the end.'

Alex looked at the stars. To the west was the faintly glowing zodiacal light, and in the south the two ghostly patches of the Magellanic Clouds. Orion was rising in the east, upside down. He nodded slowly as his mind chewed over and digested his father's words and all the things he had seen and done over the past week.

Then a thought occurred to him that had him grinning broadly. 'Dad? If you light the fire, I've got this great idea for dinner . . .'

CHRIS RYAN'S TOP SAS TACTICS ON ESCAPE AND EVASION

Every living thing leaves some kind of trail or sign, such as footprints. If you're trying to be found, you leave very noticeable signs deliberately. For instance, when Li left the plane, she did as much as possible to make sure it could be seen from the air, and she indicated clearly to would-be rescuers which way she was going.

But even without these, an experienced tracker could follow your every move. If you don't want to be found, you have to cover these marks, leave as few as possible, or throw your pursuers off your trail.

During the first Gulf War I needed all my skills to escape through 300km of enemy desert. More recently I put all my skills to the test again evading an elite tracking team in BBC TV's *Hunting Chris Ryan.*

SO HOW DO YOU DISAPPEAR?

The first thing to do is to get as far away from your pursuers as possible before they know you've gone. But once you are being followed, take great care. If you smash through the undergrowth, you may make great progress but you will be leaving clues left, right and centre. Also, you will be unable to hear if anyone is barging along after you!

If you've crashed in a plane or truck, the normal survival rule is to *stay with it*. But if you're on the run it will betray your position. *Get away*, taking any supplies you can. The less time you have to spend looking for food and water, the more time you can spend escaping.

SCENT

If your pursuers have tracker dogs, all is not lost. It's not the dog you're trying to beat, but the handler. You want to make the handler give up. They will probably find your trail easily, so make it confusing. Do a ninety-degree turn for no reason. Although it will be crystal clear to the dog what you've done, the handler will be baffled. If he/she starts getting annoyed, the dog will stop performing for him/her.

Most of us know that a river or stream will mask scent, but your pursuers will look for where you got in and out. To keep them guessing, get out a couple of times and leave a false trail before doubling back on your tracks.

The handler will not be nearly as fit as the dog, so try to exhaust him. When we were evading tracker dogs in the SAS we used to run fast for as long as possible, to tire the handler out. We chose arduous terrain such as marshes and bogs. We'd freak him out by leading them through thickets that might cut the dog's eyes, and over broken glass. Better still, we'd lead them into a snare. This wastes time while they get free, and makes them very cautious about following further. If you can lay a snare you might leave explosives for them later.

Even without tracker dogs, some smells can give you away in certain environments. In remote areas such as the jungle or the outback, toiletries such as after-shave lotion, scented soap or even toothpaste are very noticeable. They will tell a pursuer someone is there. People don't notice each other's body odour in those conditions – trust me, you can go without deodorant for a few days!

TURNING INVISIBLE

The human eye is very good at picking up movement. Avoid roads, where you may be spotted without even realizing it, and terrain that leaves obvious tracks, such as snow. Keep to the side of open ground, even if it means making a detour. It's easier to vanish in a wood than in an open plain.

If you come to a natural bottleneck, such as a gateway, beware of traps. A skilled chase team will anticipate places you cannot avoid and try to catch you out. Travel at night if at all possible.

Your silhouette is a give-away. Keep off ridges and away from backgrounds that may show you up. Camouflage your profile using vegetation and smear your face with mud or berry juice. Do a thorough job – don't forget that behind your ears and the back of your neck show up just as much as the rest of you. If you're dark-skinned like Amber, you may still need some camouflage to cut down the natural shine of the skin. The more you blend in, the harder you are to see.

Your footprints are an obvious sign for pursuers. Logos on soles etc may make it very easy to narrow down which prints are yours. But other details also make an individual print easier to identify – worn or unworn heels, the distribution of weight and so on. Try walking in mud to see how distinctive your own prints are. If you limp like Pirroni it makes your tracks very easy to recognize! The key point here is to try to leave as few prints as possible, although sometimes it is unavoidable – unless you have the power to levitate! If you have time, erase your prints; during *Hunting Chris Ryan* in Botswana I used a branch to wipe away prints I had left in sandy ground.

Trackers will also look for disturbed soil or vegetation. These signs are as obvious to a pursuer as a footprint. When most vegetation is stepped on, dragged or cut, the lighter underside of the leaves shows up. Not only can your pursuers tell you've been there, they can tell which way you were going. If you come to terrain like this, you may want to double back and choose a different route. On the other hand, you may decide it's an excellent opportunity to lay a false trail! Remember, though, that that will take extra time.

Be careful moving near thorny plants. There are lots in the jungle and you might leave tell-tale scraps of clothing behind. Worse still, you might get truly stuck. When I was in the Australian rainforest with the SAS, the bane of our lives was a charming plant known as the lawyer vine or *wait-a-while*. If you got caught on it, the worst thing you could do was struggle because you'd tear your uniform to shreds – and probably cut yourself badly. One of your mates had to pull each barb out, one by one. But we used to leave it in the paths of anyone who was pursuing us. It's nature's own barbed wire.

Of course, it goes without saying that litter is also a dead give-away. If you have to discard rubbish or equipment, bury it – and disguise the hole.

SOUND

If your pursuer can't see you, they will certainly be listening out for you. You can't help making some sounds as you move, but you can mask them by staying close to something else that is noisy, such as a stream. Otherwise, try to move smoothly and carefully, keeping an eye open for obstacles before you meet them so that your noiseless progress isn't suddenly ruined when you tumble spectacularly over a hidden log.

Even if you're being as quiet as you can, wildlife may give you away. Animals may stampede and birds may take off in a squawking flock. Alternatively, all the sounds around you may suddenly cease – which will be rather noticeable in a noisy environment such as a jungle. Some birds and animals have distinctive warning cries, which experienced trackers may know. Of course experienced trackers will also know that these signs may be caused by a predator and are not necessarily a person on the run. But someone who's looking for you will use any clues they can.

GOING INTO HIDING

You may need to find shelter to rest or hole up until darkness. Concealment is the name of the game. If you're constructing a shelter, make sure it doesn't stand out or have a silhouette that doesn't blend in with the surroundings. Although it may be tempting to use old buildings, don't. Even if they are very run-down, it's the first place your pursuers will look. Thick, impenetrable vegetation makes the best cover, but be careful not to disturb it getting in or out.

You can also reduce the chances of being found by hiding somewhere truly off-putting. When I was making *Hunting Chris Ryan* in the Honduran jungle I hid from the hunter force in a pit of sewage. They didn't want to spend much time searching for me in there! (It will also help confuse any tracker dogs, too. But don't try to venture through a built-up area afterwards or someone is bound to notice you!)

Don't just go straight to your chosen hidey-hole and stop. Walk past it and come back in a loop so you can see if people are following. Also make sure you have at least two escape routes in case you're ambushed when you're in there.

Don't stay for more than 24 hours in one hide. When you're holed up, sleep or plan your next move. Visiting wildlife might be useful for your next meal. When I was on a mission in Botswana, the bushmen showed us all sorts of grubs and beetles we could eat. Avoid caterpillars and centipedes, but insects and worms are a rich source of protein – although they may not look too appetizing. Remove the wings and carapace of insects, and starve any worms or snails for a day before you eat them, in case they have eaten something that doesn't agree with you. Grubs from wood-boring plants, such as the witchetty grub, are also very nutritious, although they look disgusting. These delicacies can all be eaten raw or cooked – but be sure that if you light a fire it isn't going to give you away – or set your hide ablaze!

If you plan to be in an area for a few days, you could set up some snares and traps to catch bigger wildlife and fish. If using traps, place them out of sight on land and under water in rivers. Remember that if one of your pursuers finds your traps, they will know you are nearby. Don't forget to dismantle your traps when you move on.

WATER

Water is absolutely essential to survival – far more so than food. If you have to choose between spending time on catching food or finding water, go for the water. In hot climates such as the rainforest and the desert, you are sweating all the time and must replace the water. If you don't, you will start to experience a range of uncomfortable symptoms, such as nausea, sleepiness, disorientation and headache and will die within days. Sometimes very dehydrated people don't feel thirsty, so you can't rely on your sense of thirst to tell you it's time to find water. So drink all the time.

Take care when gathering water from natural sources such as streams. The ground on the banks is often soft and before you know it you will be leaving nice, deep prints. Stand on logs and rocks if possible.

Always boil water before drinking it – you will

lose more fluid through an attack of the runs than you take in through drinking!

Alpha Force were lucky enough to be with an Aboriginal who knew how to find water-bearing roots. There are several plants in outback Australia that yield drinkable water, but unless you have been shown how to find them you may spend a lot of time and energy looking for them.

It is also possible to get water from animals. Alpha Force are shown how the *Cyclorana platy-cephala* frog carries a bladder of water. To drink it, put the frog's mouth to yours and squeeze gently. But as with the plants, you have to know what's what. Some frogs have poisonous skin and if you go kissing any old one you might get a nasty surprise.

If you really have to, you can get water from the eyeballs and stomachs of herbivores such as cattle and camels. If you wring out the stomach contents you should find quite a lot of liquid. You have to be pretty desperate, and it tastes disgusting, but a survival situation is no time to be squeamish. Only use animals that are freshly killed, though – you might catch something nasty from a rather old corpse.

Be safe!

Chris Ryan

Random House Children's Books and Chris Ryan would like to make it clear that these tips are for use in a serious situation only, where your life may be at risk. We cannot accept any liability for inappropriate usage in normal conditions.

About the Author

Chris Ryan joined the SAS in 1984 and has been involved in numerous operations with the regiment. During the Gulf War, he was the only member of an eight-man team to escape from Iraq, three colleagues being killed and four captured. It was the longest escape and evasion in the history of the SAS. For this he was awarded the Military Medal. He wrote about his remarkable escape in the adult bestseller *The One That Got Away* (1995), which was also adapted for screen.

He left the SAS in 1994 and is now the author of a number of bestselling thrillers for adults. His work in security takes him around the world and he has also appeared in a number of television series, most recently *Hunting Chris Ryan*, in which his escape and evasion skills were demonstrated to the max. The *Alpha Force* titles are his first books for young readers.

If you enjoyed this book, look out for the next in the Alpha Force adventures, *Hunted*, coming in November:

ALPHA FORCE

Target: Ivory Hunters

HUNTED

Alpha Force head to Zambia to compete in an extreme sports contest. When they discover a horrifying threat to the local wildlife, they snap into action, only to find themselves facing a desperate battle with a ruthless band of ivory poachers who are prepared to shoot to kill. The team freefall into danger . . .

ISBN 0 099 46425 X

If you enjoyed this book, you might like to read the first Alpha Force adventure:

ALPHA FORCE

Mission: Survival

SURVIVAL

Alex, Li, Paulo, Hex and Amber are five teenagers on board a sailing ship crewed by young people from all over the world. Together they are marooned on a desert island. And together they must face the ultimate test – survival! Battling against unbelievable dangers – from killer komodo dragons to sharks and modern-day pirates – the five must combine all their knowledge and skills if they are to stay alive.

The team – Alpha Force – is born . . .

ISBN 0 099 43924 7

If you enjoyed this book look out for others in the series:

ALPHA FORCE

Target: Drug Rat

RAT-CATCHER

Alpha Force are an elite team of five highly-skilled individuals brought together to battle injustice. Together they join a covert SAS operation in South America, fighting to catch an evil drugs baron. To gain information, they infiltrate a tight-knit community of street kids then head into the isolated mountains where a terrifying and twisted hunt is to test their individual skills to the max . . .

ISBN 0 099 43925 5

If you enjoyed this book look out for others in the series:

ALPHA FORCE

Target: Toxic Waste

HOSTAGE

Alpha Force are five teenagers who have formed a highly-skilled squad to help in the international fight against evil. Flying to Northern Canada to investigate reports of illegal dumping of toxic waste, the team must dive into an icy river, cross the harsh landscape on snowmobiles and mobilize their caving skills to complete their mission. But they need all their courage and determination when they come face-to-face with a man who is ready to kill – or take a hostage – to stop them.

The team face their toughest challenge yet . . .

ISBN 0 099 43927 1